"You Belong To Me, My Jasmine," Tariq Murmured. "This Is Forever."

Jasmine laid her head against his chest and swallowed her tears. At one time, she would have crawled on her hands and knees across broken glass for the promise of forever with this man. But forever with a Tariq who didn't love her—who would *never* love her—wasn't enough.

The obstacles in her path had grown to almost insurmountable proportions. Convincing Tariq of her loyalty would not be enough. He might eventually forgive her for not fighting for their love in the past. But would he ever forgive the second staggering blow to his warrior's pride?

What would happen when he learned the secret that had made her turn away from him all those years ago…?

D1018530

Dear Reader,

When it comes to passion, Silhouette Desire has exactly what you need. This month's offerings include Cindy Gerard's *The Librarian's Passionate Knight,* the next installment of DYNASTIES: THE BARONES. A naive librarian gets swept off her feet by a dashing Barone sibling—who could ask for anything more? But more we do have, with another story about attractive and wealthy men, from Anne Marie Winston. *Billionaire Bachelors: Gray* is a deeply compelling story about a man who gets a second chance at life—and maybe the love of a lifetime.

Sheri WhiteFeather is back this month with the final story in our LONE STAR COUNTRY CLUB trilogy. *The Heart of a Stranger* will leave you breathless when a man with a sordid past gets a chance for ultimate redemption. Launching a new series this month is Kathie DeNosky with *Lonetree Ranchers: Brant.* When a handsome rancher helps a damsel in distress, all his defenses come crashing down and the fun begins.

Silhouette Desire is pleased to welcome two brand-new authors. Nalini Singh's *Desert Warrior* is an intense, emotional read with an alpha hero to die for. And Anna DePalo's *Having the Tycoon's Baby*, part of our ongoing series THE BABY BANK, is a sexy romp about one woman's need for a child and the sexy man who grants her wish—but at a surprising price.

There's plenty of passion rising up here in Silhouette Desire this month. So dive right in and enjoy.

Melissa Jeglinski

Melissa Jeglinski
Senior Editor
Silhouette Desire

Please address questions and book requests to:
Silhouette Reader Service
U.S.: 3010 Walden Ave., P.O. Box 1325, Buffalo, NY 14269
Canadian: P.O. Box 609, Fort Erie, Ont. L2A 5X3

Desert Warrior
Nalini Singh

Published by Silhouette Books
America's Publisher of Contemporary Romance

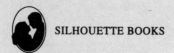

SILHOUETTE BOOKS

ISBN 0-373-76529-0

DESERT WARRIOR

Copyright © 2003 by Nalini Singh

All rights reserved. Except for use in any review, the reproduction
or utilization of this work in whole or in part in any form by any
electronic, mechanical or other means, now known or hereafter
invented, including xerography, photocopying and recording, or in
any information storage or retrieval system, is forbidden without
the written permission of the editorial office, Silhouette Books,
233 Broadway, New York, NY 10279 U.S.A.

All characters in this book have no existence outside the imagination of
the author and have no relation whatsoever to anyone bearing the same
name or names. They are not even distantly inspired by any individual
known or unknown to the author, and all incidents are pure invention.

This edition published by arrangement with Harlequin Books S.A.

® and TM are trademarks of Harlequin Books S.A., used under license.
Trademarks indicated with ® are registered in the United States Patent
and Trademark Office, the Canadian Trade Marks Office and in other
countries.

Visit Silhouette at www.eHarlequin.com

Printed in U.S.A.

NALINI SINGH

has always wanted to be a writer. Along the way to her dream, she obtained degrees in both the arts and law (because being a starving writer didn't appeal). After a short stint as a lawyer, she sold her first book and from that point, there was no going back. Now an escapee from the corporate world, she is looking forward to a lifetime of writing, interspersed with as much travel as possible. Nalini loves to hear from readers. Please write to her c/o Silhouette Books, 233 Broadway, Suite 1001, New York, NY 10279.

To Mum, Dad and the Amazing FMP, for Everything

One

"Do not put even one foot on Zulheil soil unless you are ready to stay forever. You will not get past the airport gates before I kidnap you!"

Hands trembling, Jasmine skirted around the small groups of people in the waiting area and headed for the glass doors that would lead her out of the airport, and into Tariq's land.

"Madam." A dark hand fell next to hers on the handle of the luggage trolley.

Startled, she looked up into the smiling face of a man who appeared to be an airport official. "Yes?" Her heart started to pound in a mixture of hope and fear.

"You are going the wrong way. The taxis and hire cars are on the other side." He gestured toward a long corridor leading to another set of glass doors. Desert sands glittered in the distance.

"Oh." She felt foolish. Of course Tariq wouldn't complete his threat so literally. He'd been angry enough to scare her when he'd warned her against coming to his land. Now, Tariq was a cool, controlled man, whom she'd seen a number of times on television, leading peace talks between warring Arab states. Her Tariq was now Tariq al-Huzzein Donovan Zamanat, the Sheik of Zulheil, the leader of his people.

"Thank you," she managed to say. When she began to move again, the pale blue fabric of her ankle-length dress swished around her legs in time with her steps.

"It is my pleasure. I will escort you to the vehicles."

"That's very kind. What about the other travelers?"

The corners of the stranger's eyes crinkled. "But madam, you were the only foreigner on this flight."

Jasmine blinked, thinking back over the trip. All she could remember were lilting vowels and flowing hands, beautiful sloe-eyed women and protective Arabian men.

"I didn't realize," she admitted.

"Zulheil has been closed to visitors."

"But *I'm* a visitor." She stopped, wondering if it was too much to hope that Tariq would actually kidnap her. No sane woman would want to be captured by a desert sheik who held her in contempt, but she was long past logic and sanity.

Her guide paused, and she could have sworn that he blushed under his golden skin. "It...Zulheil began letting in people again this last week."

At his graceful wave, she started to push the cart down the marbled floor once more. "Was it closed because of mourning?" Her voice was quiet, respectful.

"Yes. The loss of our sheik and his beloved wife was a tragic blow to our people." His eyes momentarily darkened with pain. "But we have a good sheik in their only son. Sheik Tariq will lead us out of the darkness."

Jasmine's heart skipped a beat at Tariq's name. From somewhere she found the strength to ask, "He's ruling alone, your new sheik?"

If the man told her that Tariq had taken a wife during the period of media blackout since his parents' deaths, she'd get on the next plane out of Zulheil. Even now, her lungs protested every breath she took, and she hung on the edge of control.

The look her guide threw her was assessing. He nodded sharply, but waited until they were outside before speaking. The harsh heat of the desert hit Jasmine like a physical slap, but she stood firm. Wilting was not an option, not when this was her last chance.

There was a black limousine parked at the curb. She'd started to move away from it when her guide halted her.

"That is your taxi."

"That's definitely not a taxi." Hope, she understood, came in many forms. Hers had arrived in the shape of a long, sleek piece of gleaming machinery.

"Zulheil is rich, madam. These are our taxis."

She wondered if he expected her to believe that. Biting her lip to muffle the slightly hysterical urge to giggle, she nodded and let him put her cases into the trunk. She waited, heart pounding and mouth dry with anticipation, until he came around to the back passenger door.

"Madam?"

"Yes?"

"You asked if our sheik rules alone. The answer is yes. Some say it is because his heart has been broken." His voice was a low whisper.

Jasmine gasped. Before she could continue the conversation, he swung open the limo door. Her mind in a whirl, she stepped inside the luxurious air-conditioned interior.

The door shut.

"You really did it," she whispered to the man sitting across from her, his long legs encroaching on her space.

Tariq leaned forward, his hands on his knees. The darkness inside the limo threw the sharp lines of his face into vivid relief. None of the softness she'd seen in her Tariq was present in this hardened stranger.

"Did you doubt me, my Jasmine?"

Her body went into delayed shock at the sound of his voice. It was deep and compelling. Beautiful and dangerous. Familiar yet…different. "No."

Tariq frowned. "And yet you are here."

She bit her lower lip again and drew in a ragged breath. His eyes, deceptively dark in the confines of the vehicle, were fixed on her like those of a predator waiting to pounce. The opaque partition between passengers and driver was raised, further collapsing the space, leaving her nowhere to turn.

"Yes. I'm here." The car moved off at that moment, unsettling her precarious balance. She fell forward and barely caught herself on the edge of the seat. Tariq's arms came around her anyway and he lifted her into his lap.

Jasmine clutched at his wide shoulders, the fine material of his white tunic crumpling under her fingers, but she didn't fight, not even when he gripped her chin with his fingers and forced her to meet his gaze. He was so angry. She could see the turbulence in his vivid green eyes.

"Why are you here?" He tightened his hold around her when the car bounced over something on the road. His muscled body was so much bigger than hers that Jasmine felt surrounded, overwhelmed. But still she didn't fight.

"Because you needed me."

His laugh was a harsh, ragged echo of pain that hurt her inside. "Or have you come to have a liaison with an exotic man, before you marry the one your family has chosen?" With an oath, he dumped her unceremoniously back into her seat.

Jasmine pushed her fiery plait over her shoulder and lifted her chin. "I don't have liaisons." His distrust of her was clear, but she refused to let that silence her.

"No," he agreed, his voice cold. "You would have to have a heart to experience passion."

Her already fragile confidence was shaken by the direct hit. All her life she'd struggled to be special enough to deserve love and acceptance. Now it appeared that even Tariq, the one person who'd ever treated her as if she were worth cherishing, found her wanting.

"You can't hold a man like Tariq. He'll forget you the minute some glamourpuss princess comes along."

Uninvited, Sarah's spiteful words from four years ago burst into Jasmine's mind. Back then, they'd delivered the last emotional blow to her belief in herself, coming from an older sister who knew so much more about men. What if it hadn't just been spite? What if Sarah had been right?

When Jasmine had made the fateful decision to find Tariq again, she'd been uncertain of her ability to reach the man she'd known. How could she hope to reach the man he'd become? Buffeted by doubt, she turned and stared out the tinted windows. There was nothing to see but endless desert.

Strong fingers on her jaw forced her attention back to the panther lounging opposite her. His green-eyed gaze caught her own and held her in thrall. "I will keep you, my Jasmine." It was a statement, not a question.

"And if I don't wish to be..." She paused, unable to think of the right word.

"Owned?" Tariq suggested in a silky whisper.

Jasmine swallowed. A part of her was terrified of the dark fury she saw swirling in his eyes, but she'd come too far to fall victim to her fears now. "Like a slave?" Her voice was husky, her lips parched. However, she didn't dare moisten them with her tongue, afraid of how Tariq would react.

He narrowed his eyes. "You think I am such a barbarian?"

"I think you're going out of your way to give me that impression," she retorted, before she could caution herself not to bait the panther.

The corners of his lips tilted upward in a slight curve. "Ah, I had forgotten."

"What?" She lifted a hand to his wrist and tried to break his hold on her jaw. It proved impossible. Under her touch, his pulse beat in a slow, seductive rhythm that promised her both exotic pleasures and darkest fury.

"That the fire of your hair does not lie." He moved his thumb over her lower lip and frowned. "Your lips are dry. Moisten them."

Jasmine scowled at the command. "And if I don't?"

He lifted one brow in response to the defiance in her tone. "Then I shall do it for you."

Betraying color stained her cheeks at the erotic image of

Tariq moistening her lips. His intense gaze made her feel like
a tasty morsel he'd be only too happy to devour. Breathing in
shallow gasps, she flicked out her tongue and wet her lips.

"Better." His approval was apparent in the deepening timbre of his voice and the way his thumb slowly swept over her
lower lip, now soft and wet. When he abruptly set her free,
surprise kept her perched on the edge of her seat for a moment,
leaning toward him. Sanity returned with a shock. Face
flushed, she scrambled back and across the seat until she was
in the opposite corner of the car.

"Where are you taking me?"

"Zulheina."

"The capital?"

"Yes."

"Where in Zulheina?" She refused to back down despite
his repressive monosyllabic replies.

"To my palace." He lifted one foot and placed it next to
her right hip, effectively caging her against the door. "Tell
me, my Jasmine, what have you been doing these four years?"

It was clear that he wasn't going to answer any more questions. Jasmine bit back her frustration, wanting to push but
aware that she was on very shaky ground. "I was studying."

"Ah, the business management degree." His words were a
soft taunt, a reminder of the times she'd cried on his shoulder,
sobbing out her dislike of the subject.

"No." *There,* she thought, *let him suffer for a minute.*

He moved and suddenly he was sitting next to her, his
shoulders blocking her vision, his legs caging her in the corner. He wasn't the one suffering.

"No?" His deep voice evoked memories of huskier tones
and sensual laughter. "Your family let you change?"

"They had no choice." She'd followed their dictates and
cut herself off from Tariq, but it had almost destroyed her.
Her weak state had alarmed even her family, and no one had
commented when she'd switched studies. By the time they'd
tried to change her mind, she'd grown up. Disillusionment

with the selfishness of those she'd trusted had followed fast
on the heels of her sorrow.

"What did you study? Hmm?" He curved one big hand
round her neck in a blatantly possessive gesture. The heat from
his body swirled around her.

"Do you have to sit so close?" she blurted out.

For the first time, he smiled. It was a smile full of teeth,
the smile of a predator tempting his prey to venture out into
the darkness. "Do I bother you, Mina?"

He'd called her Mina. She remembered the way he'd always
shortened her name to Mina when he'd been coaxing her to
do something, usually involving kissing him until she felt like
liquid honey inside. He hadn't needed to coax much. One look
of sexy invitation, the husky whisper of her name against her
lips, and she'd softened like a sigh in the wind.

When she didn't answer, he leaned down and nuzzled her
neck, his warm breath seeming to burrow through her skin and
into her bones. He'd always loved to touch. She'd relished his
affection, but right now it was making her more off balance
than she already was.

"Tariq, please."

"What do you want, Mina?"

Jasmine swallowed. He traced the movement down her
throat with his thumb. "Space."

He raised his head. "No. You have had four years of space.
Now you are mine."

His intensity was almost frightening. As an eighteen-year-
old, she'd been unable to cope with his sheer, charismatic
power. Though he was only five years older than her, his
strength and determination even then had been enough to command unswerving loyalty from his people. Now, four years
later, she could see that he'd grown impossibly stronger, impossibly more charismatic. However, she was no longer a shel-
tered young girl, and she had to learn to cope with Tariq if
she wanted a future with him.

Holding his gaze, she lifted her hand and placed it over the
one curled around her neck. When she tugged, he released her,

his curiosity apparent in the quizzical look in his green eyes. Raising his hand to her cheek, she turned her face to drop a single kiss on his palm. His breath grew harsh, loud in the confines of the car.

"I studied fashion design." His skin was warm against her lips, his masculine scent an irresistible aphrodisiac.

"You have changed."

"For the better."

"That remains to be seen." His eyes narrowed. The hand against her cheek tightened. "Who taught you this?"

"What?" Shivers threatened to whisper down her spine at the sound of that dark, rough tone.

"This play with my hand and your lips." His jaw could have been carved out of granite.

"You did." It was the truth. "Remember the time you took me to the Waitomo caves? As the canoe floated in the glow-worm grotto, you picked up my hand and you kissed it just so." She moved her head, and he loosened his hold enough to allow her to repeat the soft caress.

When she looked up, she knew that he'd remembered, but his features remained stony and his eyes boiled with emotions she didn't have the experience to identify.

"There have been others?"

"What?"

"Other men have touched you?"

"No. Only you."

He curved his hand around to tug at her plait, arching her neck and making her vulnerable to him. "Do not lie to me. I will know," he growled.

He was threatening to overwhelm her. In response, she relaxed into the exposed position that he'd engineered and slid her arms around his neck. "I will know, too," she said quietly. Under her fingers, his hair was soft, tempting her to stroke. Below that was the living heat of his skin.

His jaw firmed. "What will you know?"

"If you've let other women touch you."

Tariq's eyes widened. "When did you become fierce, Mina?

You were always so biddable.'' She knew he was taunting her with the way she'd let her family control her life, even to the extent of ignoring her heart.

"I had to grow claws to survive.''

"And am I supposed to be frightened of your puny claws?'' He raised one dark brow, daring her.

Deliberately, Jasmine sank her fingernails into the back of his neck. She forgot that she was goading a panther. To her surprise, her panther didn't seem to mind her claws. He smiled down at her, a dangerous, tempting smile.

"I would like to feel those claws on my back, Mina,'' he whispered. "When you are in your place—flat on your back, under me—then I will.''

"In my place?'' Jasmine jerked out of his hold. When he continued to loom over her, his body crowding her against the door, she pushed at his chest. Masculine heat seared her through the fine fabric. "Move, you…you male!''

"No, Mina.'' He put one hand against her cheek and turned her toward him. "I will no longer follow your commands like a dog on a leash. From this day forth, you will follow mine.''

He held her in place as his lips descended over hers. He needn't have bothered. Jasmine was transfixed by the raw pain she'd glimpsed on his face, before his shields had risen. She'd done this to her panther. It was, she acknowledged, his right to demand restitution.

Two

Tariq couldn't fight the driving, primitive urge to taste Mina, to claim her in this small way. Not even the knowledge that she was feeling overwhelmed and trapped could halt him. He tried to be gentle in his possession, but he hungered too much to stop. Then small, feminine hands clutched at his nape, holding him to her, inciting him. The painful craving he'd leashed for years battered at his control, pleading for freedom. He wanted to gorge on Mina. To feast on Mina.

Not now, he decided.

When he took her, he wanted hours, days, weeks in which to linger over her. But that long-suppressed craving had to be fed something, or it would shatter the bonds he'd imposed in order to keep from being eaten alive. Anger threatened to flame at the edge of his consciousness as he crushed her soft lips under his. He'd kill any man who'd dared to touch her. He would never forgive her if she'd allowed a single caress.

Mina was his.

And this time, he wouldn't let her forget.

In his arms, she shivered, and the simmering need inside him threatened to take complete command. He stroked his tongue across the seam of her lips. She opened at once. The taste of her was an elixir, a drug he'd starved for for years. His feelings for her were as wild and chaotic as a desert storm. How dare she leave him? How dare she take four years to return? When she gasped for breath, he breathed into her mouth, feeding her even as he took from her.

"No one else has touched you." He found some peace in that. Not much, but enough to rein in the beast.

"And," Jasmine responded in shocked surprise, "no one else has touched *you*."

He smiled that predator's smile. "I'm very hungry, Mina."

Jasmine felt her body begin to react as it always had to Tariq's dark sensuality. "Hungry?"

"Very." He was stroking her neck with his thumb in an absent fashion, feeling the vibration as she spoke.

"I need time." She was unprepared for the reality of the man he'd become. Dark. Beautiful. Magnificent. Angry.

He raised his eyes from his perusal of her throat. "No. I am no longer willing to indulge you."

She had no response to that flat statement. Four years ago, Tariq had delighted in letting her have her way. She'd never had to fight this warrior. Back then, he'd been careful with her innocence, but when he'd touched her, Jasmine hadn't felt like an outcast. She'd felt cherished. Today, she didn't feel that beautiful but fragile emotion. Tariq wasn't acting like a lover, but rather a conqueror with his prize. The true depth of what she'd lost was only now becoming clear.

He moved and set her free, but remained on her side of the car, one arm slung negligently over the back of her seat. "So, you have been studying fashion design."

"Yes."

"You wish to be a famous designer?" He threw her a look full of male amusement.

Jasmine bristled. Though used to her family mocking her

dreams, she'd never expected it from Tariq. "Why is that funny?" She aimed a scowl at his savagely masculine features.

He chuckled. "Sheathe your claws, Mina. I simply cannot see you designing those ridiculous things on the catwalks. Your dresses wouldn't be see-through, hmm, displaying to the world treasures that should only be viewed by one man?"

She blushed at his heated gaze, ridiculously pleased that he wasn't laughing at her.

"Tell me," he commanded.

"I want to design feminine things." Her dream was real to her, no matter what anyone said, but until this moment, no one's opinion had truly mattered. "These days, the male designers seem to have an incredibly macabre idea of the female form. Their models are flat boards with not a curve in sight."

"Ah." It was a wholly male sound.

She looked up, suspicious. "Ah, what?"

Tariq spread one possessive hand over her abdomen. She gasped. "You're full of curves, Mina."

"I never pretended to be a sylph."

His warm breath close to her ear startled her. "You misunderstand. I'm delighted by your curves. They'll cushion me perfectly."

Biting hurt turned to red-hot embarrassment and shocking desire. Blinded by longing, she barely finished her explanation. "I want to design pretty things for real women."

Tariq regarded her with a contemplative expression. "You'll be permitted to continue this."

"I'll be *permitted* to continue my work?"

"You will need something to do when I'm not with you."

She gave a frustrated little scream and shifted until her back was plastered against the door, making it possible for her to glower up at him. "You have no right to *permit* me to do anything!" She poked him in the chest with her index finger.

He captured her hand. "On the contrary, I have every right." The sudden chill in his voice stopped her.

"You are now my possession. I own you. That means I have the right to do with you as I please." This time there was no hint of humor in his expression, not even the shadow of the man she'd once known. "You would do well not to provoke me. I have no intention of being cruel, but neither will you find me a fool for your charms a second time."

When, after a frozen moment, he released her and moved back to the opposite side of the car, she gathered the shreds of her composure around her and turned to the window. Had she done this? she asked herself. Had she with her cowardice so totally destroyed the beauty of what had once been between them? She wanted to cry at the loss, but something in her, the same something that had urged her to come to him when she'd heard of his parents' deaths, refused to surrender.

Unbidden, she remembered the way he'd held her so protectively in his arms when she'd run to him, frightened by the suffocation of her home.

"Come home with me, my Jasmine. Come to Zulheil."

"I can't! My parents…"

"They seek to capture you, Mina. I would set you free."

It was a bitter irony that the very man who'd once promised her freedom was now intent on caging her.

"I was only eighteen," she exclaimed abruptly.

"You are no longer eighteen." He sounded dangerous.

"Can't you understand what it was like for me?" she pleaded, despite herself. "They were my parents and I'd only known you for six months."

"Then why did you—what is your phrase?" He paused. "Yes…why did you lead me on? Did it amuse you to have an Arab royal at your beck and call?"

He'd never been at her beck and call. At eighteen, she'd had even less self-confidence than she did now, but he'd always made her feel…important. "No! No! I didn't…."

"Enough." His voice cut through her protests like a knife. "The truth is that when your family asked you to choose, you did not choose me. You did not even tell me so *I* could fight for us. There is nothing further to say."

Jasmine was silenced. Yes, it was the truth. How could she even begin to make a man like him understand what it had been like for her? Born with a mantle of power, Tariq had never known how it felt to be crushed and belittled until he didn't know his own mind. Shrinking into her corner, she thought back to the day that had changed her forever. Her father had forbidden her to see Tariq, threatening to disown her. She'd begged on her knees but he'd made her choose.

"The Arab or your family."

He'd always called Tariq "the Arab." It wasn't racism, but something much deeper. At first she'd thought it was because they expected her to marry into another high-country farming family. Only later had she understood the ugly reality of why they'd crushed her small rebellion under their feet.

Tariq had been meant for Sarah.

Beautiful Sarah had wished to be a princess, and everyone had assumed it would happen. Except, from the moment he'd arrived, Tariq's eyes had lingered on Jasmine, the daughter who wasn't a daughter, the daughter who was a cause for shame, not celebration.

The huge spread in the hills, which had been Jasmine's home, had been in the Coleridge family for generations. As the beneficiaries of that heritage, Jasmine's parents had been used to controlling everything in their high-country kingdom and they had feared Tariq's strength of will. Added to that, his choice of Jasmine over Sarah had made him anathema. To let Jasmine have him when their darling Sarah couldn't, would have meant being continuously faced with both their failure to manipulate Tariq *and* the wrong daughter's happiness. It was ugly and it was vicious, but it was the truth. Jasmine was no longer a needy child, and couldn't pretend that they'd had her best interests at heart.

"Did you implement that irrigation system?" Her voice was softened by pain. They'd met when he'd visited New Zealand to learn about a revolutionary new watering system discovered by a neighboring family.

"It has been operating successfully for three years."

She nodded and laid her head against the seat. At eighteen, she'd made the wrong choice because she'd been terrified of losing the only people who might ever accept her, flawed as she was. A week ago, she'd turned her back on those very people and ventured out to try and recapture the glorious love she'd had with Tariq.

What would he say if she told him that she was now alone in the world?

Her father had carried out his threat and disowned her. But this time she hadn't compromised her soul in a bid for acceptance. She'd walked away, aware that she'd made an irrevocable decision. There would be no welcome back.

The only things Jasmine had in the world were her determination and a soul-deep love that had never died, but she couldn't tell Tariq that. His pity would be far worse than his anger. She'd chosen him and completely forsaken everything else. But was it too late?

"We are approaching Zulheina, if you wish to look."

Grateful for a chance to escape the distressing memories, she pressed a button by her elbow and the window rolled down. Warm air floated in, caressing her cold cheeks. "Oh, my," she whispered, distracted from her emotional agony.

Zulheina was a city of legend. Very few foreigners were ever allowed into the inner sanctum of Zulheil. Business was usually carried out in the larger town of Abraz, in the north. She could see why the people of Zulheil guarded this place with such zeal. It was utterly magnificent.

Fragile-seeming minarets reached for the heavens, illusions that touched the indigo-blue sky. The single river that ran through Zulheil, and eventually fed out into the sea, passed by in a foaming rush. The white marble of the nearest buildings reflected its tumbling, crystalline beauty.

"It's like something out of a fairy tale." She was fascinated by the way the water flowed under them as they drove over the bridge and entered the city proper.

"It is now your home." Tariq's words were a command.

Strange and wondrous smells drifted to her on the warm breeze. Sounds followed, then the vibrant living colors of the people as the limousine passed through a busy marketplace.

Hard male fingers encircled the soft flesh of her upper arm. Startled, she faced Tariq. His green eyes were hooded, hiding his emotions from her. "I said that it is now your home. You have nothing to say to that?"

Home, Jasmine thought, a sense of wonder infusing her. She'd never had a real home. Her smile was luminous. "I think that it will be no hardship to call this place home." She thought the panther opposite her relaxed a little. In the next moment, she saw something out of the corner of her eye that made her gasp. "I don't believe it. It can't be true." Ignoring the firm but strangely gentle grip on her arm, she stretched her neck to peer out the window.

Rising in front of her was the most fragile-looking building she'd ever seen. It seemed to be formed out of mist and raindrops, the artistry in the carving magnificent beyond imagining. The crystal-white stone of the building seemed to glow with a pale rose luminescence that had her transfixed.

She turned to Tariq, wide-eyed, forgetting his anger in her amazement. "I could swear that building is made of Zulheil Rose."

Though Zulheil was a tiny desert sheikdom, enclosed on three sides by bigger powers, and on the fourth by the sea, it was a rich land, producing not just oil, but a beautiful, precious stone called Zulheil Rose. The striking, clear crystal with the hidden fire inside was the rarest gem on the planet, found only in Tariq's land.

"If your eyes get any bigger, my Jasmine, they'll rival the sky," Tariq teased.

Jasmine forgot the stunning building the moment she heard the quiet humor in his tone. Tariq had apparently decided to put aside his anger for the moment.

"That is your new home."

"What?" She lost any composure she might've attained.

He eyed her flushed features with amused interest. "The royal palace is indeed made of Zulheil Rose. Now you see why we do not let many foreigners into our city."

"Good grief." Earnestly, she leaned forward, unconsciously

putting her palms on his thighs for balance. "I know the crystal is harder than diamonds and impenetrable, but don't your people, um, get tempted to chip off pieces?"

His voice was rough when he answered, "The people of Zulheil are happy and well cared for. They are not tempted to lose their place in this society for money.

"And the palace is considered sacred. It was carved where it stands by the one who founded Zulheil. Never in the history of our land has anyone discovered another such concentration of the crystal. It's believed that as long as the palace stands, Zulheil will prosper."

Hard male muscles flexed under her fingers. Jasmine jerked up her head. Blood rushed through her veins to stain her cheeks bright red. Flustered, she removed her hands and scrambled back into her seat.

"That, Mina," Tariq said, as they came to a stop in the inner courtyard of the palace, "is something you're permitted to do at will."

Hot with a combination of embarrassment and desire, she muttered, "What?"

"Touch me."

She sucked in her breath. It was clear that while Tariq had been prepared to wait for intimacy when she'd been eighteen, he was no longer so patient.

They stepped out into the heart of the palace complex—a lush garden protected from the outside by curving walls of Zulheil Rose. From where she stood, Jasmine could see a pomegranate tree heavy with fruit in one corner of the garden. A fig tree dominated the other. Bright, luxuriant and glossy flowers spread like a carpet in either direction.

"It's like a page of the *Arabian Nights* come to life." Any second now she expected a peacock to come strutting out.

"These gardens are opened every Friday to my people. At that time I meet with those who would talk with me."

Jasmine frowned. "Just like that?"

Beside her, Tariq tightened his clasp on her hand, his big body shifting to dominate her field of vision. "You do not approve of my meeting with my people?'' The bright sunlight made his hair glitter like black diamonds.

"Not that. From what I've read, your people adore you." Pausing, she turned her head to avoid his penetrating gaze. "I was thinking about your safety."

"Would you miss me, my Jasmine, if I was gone?" The question escaped Tariq's iron control, betraying emotions he refused to acknowledge.

"What a thing to ask! Of course I'd miss you."

Yet she'd walked away from him without a backward look, while he'd bled from the heart. "It has always been done this way in my land. Zulheil is small but prosperous. It will only stay that way if the people are content. None would hurt me because they know I will listen to their concerns."

"What about outsiders?" Her hand clenched around his.

He was unable to restrain his smile, seeing in her intent expression echoes of the bright young girl who'd claimed his soul. "The minute a foreigner enters our borders, we know."

"Your driver tried to convince me this was a taxi." Her gentle laughter was as light as the desert dawn.

At the happy sound, something deep inside Tariq was tempted to awaken. He had ached for her for so long. Ruthlessly, he crushed the urge. This time, he would not give Jasmine either his trust or his heart. Not when the scars from the hurt she'd inflicted in the past had yet to heal.

"Mazeel is a good driver, but not the best of actors." He looked up at the sound of approaching footsteps.

"Your Highness." A familiar pair of brown eyes regarded him with barely veiled disapproval. Tariq wasn't worried. Hiraz might let him see his anger, but his loyalty would keep him silent on what mattered.

"You remember Hiraz." He nodded at his chief advisor and closest friend, allowing the woman in his arms to turn.

"Of course. It's nice to see you again, Hiraz."

Hiraz bowed, his manner stiff and formal. "Madam."

"Please, call me Jasmine."

Under Tariq's hand, her back felt incredibly fragile. He

didn't fight the surge of fierce protectiveness that thundered through him. However angry he was with her, Mina was his to protect. *His.*

"Hiraz does not approve of my plans concerning you, Mina." His words were a subtle warning.

"Your Highness, I would speak with you." Hiraz blinked in understanding, but his stance remained stiff. "Your uncle and his entourage have arrived, as have all the others."

"And he only calls me Your Highness when he wants to annoy me," Tariq murmured. "It is not the address of our people." It took an effort to keep his tone even after the blithely delivered message. The arrival of those who would stand witness to the events of this night, brought his plans one step closer to fruition.

Hiraz sighed and relaxed, unable to continue on in such an unfamiliar way. "So you actually did it." His gaze settled on Jasmine. "Do you understand what he has planned?"

"Enough." Tariq made the words an autocratic warning.

Hiraz merely lifted a brow and moved aside. He fell into step beside them as they entered the palace.

"What have you planned?" Jasmine asked.

"I will tell you later."

"When?"

"Jasmine." His quiet, implacable tone usually commanded instant obedience.

"Tariq." At the unexpected echo, he paused and turned, to find Mina scowling up at him.

Hiraz's chuckle provided welcome respite from the sudden shock of recognizing that Jasmine was no longer the fragile girl of his memories. "I see that she has grown up. Good. She will not be easy to control. You would crush a weak woman."

"She will do as I say."

Jasmine wanted to protest at the way they were ignoring her presence, but Tariq's dark expression stole her faltering courage. He'd humored her in the final minutes of the journey, but the man in front of her was the Sheik of Zulheil. And she didn't know this powerful stranger.

Inside, the palace was surprisingly comfortable, with nothing ornate or overdone. Light came in through lots of tiny carved windows, bathing the rooms in sunlight lace. Though beautiful, it was very much a home. Jasmine was still admiring her surroundings when a woman dressed in a long flowing dress in a shade of pale green materialized at her elbow.

"You will go with Mumtaz," Tariq decreed. He lifted their clasped hands and kissed Jasmine's wrist, his gaze locked with hers. Her blood raced through her body, frenetic with the effect of the simple caress. "I will see you in two hours." Then he was gone, striding down the corridor with Hiraz.

Three

——

Mumtaz showed her to her rooms—a suite in the southern end of the palace. While one room she was shown into had a very feminine feel, the others in the suite were full of masculine accoutrements. She commented on the fact.

"I...do not think there was enough warning of your arrival." There was an odd catch in Mumtaz's voice.

Jasmine attributed her faltering explanation to embarrassment over discussing Tariq's business. "Of course," she agreed, wishing to put the friendly woman at ease.

"Where do these doors go?" she asked, after they'd put her clothes away in the huge walk-in closet.

"Come. You will like this." Mumtaz's ebullient smile was infectious. With a flourish, she flung open the doors.

"A garden!" Under Jasmine's bare feet, the grass in the enclosed garden was soft and lush. A small fountain in the middle of the circular enclosure sent arcs of water tumbling over the Zulheil Rose carvings at its base. Benches surrounded the fountain, and were in turn encircled by millions of tiny blue flowers. A haunting fragrance drifted to her from the huge tree in the corner, which was covered with bell-shaped, blue-white blossoms.

"This is the private garden of…" Mumtaz stumbled over her words. "I am sorry, sometimes my English…"

"That's okay." Jasmine waved her hand. "I'm trying to learn the language of Zulheil, but I'm not very good yet."

Mumtaz's eyes sparkled. "I will teach you, yes?"

"Thank you! You were saying about the garden?"

Mumtaz frowned in thought. "This is the private garden of the people who live behind these…entrances." She pointed to Jasmine's door and to two other similar ones to the left. Together, they encircled three quarters of the garden. A high wall overrun with creeping vines completed the enclosure.

Jasmine nodded. "Oh, you mean it's the guests' garden."

Mumtaz shuffled her feet and gave her a smile. "You like your rooms and this garden?"

"How could I not? They're stunning."

"Good, that is good. You will stay in Zulheil?"

Jasmine looked up, surprised at her tone. "You know?"

Mumtaz sighed and took a seat on a bench near the fountain. Jasmine followed. "Hiraz is Tariq's closest friend, and as Hiraz's wife—"

"You're Hiraz's wife?" Jasmine choked. "I thought you were…never mind."

"A maid, yes?" Mumtaz smiled without rancor. "Tariq wished for you to be with someone you felt comfortable with when you arrived. I work in the palace and will be here every day. I hope you feel you can ask me for anything you need."

"Oh, yes." A little spark of warmth ignited inside Jasmine. Tariq had cared enough to arrange for this lovely woman to welcome her. "But why didn't he say anything?"

"Both he and Hiraz are terrible when they are in a temper. Tariq is angry with you, and my husband with me."

"Why is Hiraz angry with you?" Jasmine's curiosity got the better of her.

"He expects me to agree with something he and Tariq are

doing, even though he himself does not agree with Tariq.'' Before Jasmine could question her further, Mumtaz continued, ''Hiraz told me the story of what happened in your country. But it is common knowledge in Zulheil that Tariq had his heart broken by a red-haired foreigner with blue eyes.''

Jasmine blinked. ''How?''

''Hiraz would go to his grave with Tariq's secrets, but others in that party were not so…loyal,'' Mumtaz explained. ''You are a mystery, but it is good you have come now. After his parents' deaths, Tariq is much in need.''

''He's furious with me,'' she confessed.

''But you are in Zulheina. It is better to be near him even if he is angry, yes? You must learn to manage your h—''

The sudden look of distress on Mumtaz's exotic face alarmed Jasmine. ''What is it?'' she asked.

''I…I have forgotten something. Please, you must come inside.''

She followed, bemused by Mumtaz's sudden change in mood.

''A bath has been drawn for your comfort. Afterward, please wear these.'' Mumtaz pointed to clothing that had appeared on the bed.

Jasmine touched the soft and incredibly fine fabric with her fingers. It was as weightless as mist and the color of Zulheil Rose—pure white with a hidden heart of fire. There was a long flowing skirt sprinkled with tiny shards of crystal that would catch the light each time she moved. The top was a fitted bodice bordered with the same sparkling crystals. Though the long sleeves would end at her wrists, the garment itself was short and would leave her midriff bare. Multiple strands of fine gold chain lay beside the top. Clearly, they were supposed to go around her waist.

''These aren't mine,'' Jasmine whispered.

''There is a special…meal, and your clothing is not correct. This is for you as, uh…''

''A guest?'' she suggested. ''Well, I suppose if this is normal practice, then it should be okay. I just wouldn't feel comfortable wearing something so expensive otherwise.''

She had to repeatedly ensure Mumtaz that she'd be fine before the other woman would leave. "It's something formal, this dinner?" she asked, just-before Mumtaz walked out.

"Oh yes. Very formal. I will return to do your hair and make sure you look beautiful.''

As Mumtaz left, Jasmine was certain that she heard her muttering under her breath, but the delicious promise of the scented bath distracted her.

"I feel like a princess," Jasmine whispered, almost two hours after she'd entered the palace. She touched her hand to the gold circlet that Mumtaz had insisted on placing about her head. Her deep-red hair had been brushed until it shone. Now it flowed in riotous waves to the middle of her back, the fine gold strands within it complementing the simple circlet.

"Then I have done my job.'' Mumtaz laughed.

"I thought flesh wasn't meant to be shown?'' Jasmine put her hand on her abdomen. The fine gold chains about her hips were lavish and utterly seductive.

Mumtaz shook her head. "We are reserved in public only. Zulheil has no strict laws, but most women prefer modesty. In our homes with our men, it is acceptable to be more…'' She waved her hands at her own clothing. She was wearing wide-legged harem pants in a pale shade of yellow, cinched at the ankle, and a blouse fitted much like Jasmine's. However, her clothing didn't glitter with sparkling crystal shards.

"I won't be overdressed?'' Jasmine didn't want to change. She'd been imagining the look in Tariq's eyes at her appearance. Maybe he'd think her beautiful, because for the first time in her life, she felt that way.

"You are perfect. Now we must go.''

A few minutes later they entered a room full of women, all dressed in stunning costumes bursting with color. Jasmine's eyes widened. At their entry, conversation stopped. A second later, it started again in a chaotic rush. Several older women came over and invited her to sit on the cushions with them. With Mumtaz acting as a translator when necessary, Jasmine was soon laughing and talking with them as if with old friends. Something about them seemed familiar, but she couldn't put her finger on what.

The innate tensing of her body was the only warning she needed half an hour later. She looked up and found Tariq standing in the doorway. Unbidden, her legs uncurled and she stood. Silence reigned again, but this time it was full of expectancy, as if everyone was holding their breath.

He looked magnificent, dressed in a black tunic and pants, the only ornamentation being gold embroidery on the mandarin collar of the tunic. The starkness of his clothing set off the dark beauty of his features. He walked across the room and took her hand. She was vaguely aware of other men following him inside, and the rustle of cloth as the women around her stood up.

His eyes blazed with heat when he gazed at her. "You look like the heart of the Zulheil Rose," he whispered, for her ears only, his eyes on her hair. He drew back, but she felt as if she was in the center of an inferno.

"I have a question for you, my Jasmine." This time the words were crystal clear in the otherwise silent room.

She stared up at him. "Yes?"

Green fire met her. "You came to Zulheil of your own free will. Will you stay of your own free will?"

Jasmine was confused. Tariq had made it clear that he wasn't going to let her leave. Why ask her this now? However, she instinctively knew that she couldn't question him in front of witnesses, not without doing damage to his pride and standing among his people. "Yes."

Tariq's smile was quick and satisfied. He reminded her of a panther again and she suddenly felt stalked. "And will you stay *with me* of your own free will?"

The question was the trigger her mind needed. She understood what was happening, but the knowledge didn't change her answer. "I will stay," she said, and sealed her destiny.

The savage satisfaction in his eyes burned unfettered for one bright second. Then his lids lowered and hid the fire. He lifted her hand to his lips and turned it over, to lay a single kiss on the pulse beating rapidly under her skin. "I take my leave of you, my Jasmine…for now."

Then he was gone, leaving her standing, her mind in shock at what she'd just done. Giggling women came to her side and directed her back to her cushion. Jasmine caught Mumtaz's worried expression as the other woman took a seat next to her.

"You know?" The whisper reached only her ears, muffled by the buzz of conversation in the room.

Jasmine nodded. Aware that she was the center of attention, she tried to appear calm, even though her heart beat so hard she was afraid that it was going to rip out of her chest. The secret that she'd successfully buried under her love for Tariq raised its head, like a cobra readying itself to strike, taunting her with its inevitability. Unable to face his rejection, she'd planned to tell him once she was certain of her welcome in his life. Now it was too late. Much too late. How could she tell him the truth now?

"Jasmine?" Mumtaz interrupted her thoughts, reminding her of the act that had just taken place.

"When he asked me those questions…"

"I wished to tell you the truth, but they forbade it."

"And your loyalty is to Tariq." Jasmine couldn't hold the omission against Mumtaz. The other woman had done everything she could. "I thought the country was in mourning?"

"One month we have mourned, but it is part of Zulheil's culture that life conquers death. Our people would rather live joyously as an offering to those who are gone, than shroud ourselves in darkness."

Someone put a plate of sweetmeats into Jasmine's hands. She nodded an absentminded thanks at the woman, but didn't attempt to eat. Her stomach was in knots. Suddenly, she knew why the guests around her seemed so familiar. All of them had an unmistakable regal bearing that reminded her of

Tariq—of course his family would be in attendance on this night.

"Do you know what happens next?" At the negative shake of her head, Mumtaz explained. "The questions are the first step in the marriage ceremony. Second is the binding, which will be performed by an elder. The final part is the blessing, which will be sung outside. You will not see Tariq again until it is over."

Jasmine nodded. Her eyes went to the lacy window set in the middle of the dividing wall. Her future awaited on the other side. "I've never heard of such a ceremony."

"Zulheil's ways are not those of our Islamic neighbors. We follow the ancient paths," Mumtaz explained. "You truly answered him knowing the consequences?"

Jasmine drew in a deep breath. "I stepped off that plane with only one goal. I didn't expect this, but he's the only man I've ever wanted. I could never say no to him."

Mumtaz's smile was understanding. "He is angry, but he needs you. Love him, Jasmine, and teach him to love again."

Jasmine nodded. She had to teach him to love her, or she was going to spend her life as the possession of a man who didn't care about her love. A man who, unless he loved her, would reject her once she revealed her shameful secret.

By the time she stepped out of this room, she would be married to the Sheik of Zulheil.

"It is time for the binding." Mumtaz nodded toward an aged woman, clad head to toe in vibrant red, who had just entered the room.

Coming to kneel next to Jasmine, the elder smiled and picked up her right hand. "With this I bind you." She tied a beautiful red ribbon with intricate embroidery around Jasmine's wrist.

Leaning close, Jasmine saw that the embroidery was writing—flowing Arabic script. When the elder raised her wrinkled face, there was power in those dark eyes. "You will repeat my words."

Jasmine nodded jerkily.

"This binding, it be true. This binding, it be unbroken."

"This binding, it be true. This binding, it be unbroken." Her voice was a whisper, her throat clogged with the knowledge of the finality of her actions.

"With this bond, I take my life and put it in the keeping of Tariq al-Huzzein Donovan Zamanat. For ever and eternity."

Jasmine repeated the words carefully and exactly. She'd made her choice, and she would see it through, but a deep shaft of pain ran through her at the thought that her parents weren't present on this day. They'd cut her adrift with a callousness she still couldn't comprehend.

Once she'd finished, the elder picked up the other end of the ribbon and fed it through the lacy window halfway up the wall. A minute later, Jasmine felt a tug on her wrist.

Tariq had just been bound to her.

For ever and eternity.

The haunting chant that began outside seemed to echo in her soul.

Tariq stared at the small aperture that was his only window into the room where his Jasmine sat. As the blessing chant grew in volume around him, he kept his eyes trained on the opening. Images raced through his mind, competing to hold his attention.

Mina, wearing the dress of his land. He felt fierce pride in the way she'd carried herself. A princess could not have been more regal.

Mina, her red hair a fall of sunsets that beckoned him with promises of warmth. Soon he'd collect on that promise.

Mina, looking at him with eyes that betrayed her awakening sensuality. Yes, Jasmine had grown up. It would be his pleasure to teach her the secrets of the bedroom.

His need to possess her clawed at him, but underlying it was a deeper need and an even deeper hurt, things he refused to acknowledge. He allowed only a sliver of hunger to escape his control. Mina had always belonged to him, but in a few more minutes, the ties between them would become unbreakable.

Then he would claim his woman.

He was very hungry.

Tariq's words in the car refused to leave Jasmine's mind. How was she supposed to relax, knowing that a hungry panther was coming to lay claim to her? With a groan, she sat up in the huge bed in the room next to hers. Tariq's masculine presence was everywhere.

The flimsy nightgown that she'd found on the bed was scandalous as far as she was concerned. The superfine white linen fell to her ankles like a sheet of mist. It was laced with blue ribbon down to her navel, and had long sleeves tied with the same ribbon at the wrist. Thigh-high slits on either side bared her legs with every movement she made. The sleeves were also slit from wrist to shoulder, exposing her skin. All that wasn't as bad as the fact that the material was almost sheer, her nipples and the darker triangle between her legs far too visible.

"They might be reserved in public but they could give lessons in eroticism," she muttered, standing beside the bed.

Uncomfortable in the sensual clothing, she crossed to the closet, with the intention of finding a robe to throw on over it. She found a large blue silk one that was clearly Tariq's. It would have to do, she thought, and pulled it out.

"Stop."

Startled, she swiveled around. She hadn't heard him enter. Hadn't heard him move across the room. Tariq was almost upon her, his eyes hot as they skated over her body. Her gaze fixated on his naked chest. He was magnificent. His shoulders were wider than she'd imagined, the muscles thick and liquid when he moved. The ridges on his abdomen appeared hard and inflexible, pure steel under skin. The only thing saving him from nakedness was a small white towel.

"I did not give you permission to cover yourself."

Jasmine bristled at his autocratic tone. "I don't need your permission."

With a single flick of his wrist, he pushed the robe from her nerveless fingers and captured both her hands in one of his own. "You forget that I now own you. You do what I wish."

"Rubbish."

"If it comforts you, feel free to disagree," he said, magnanimous in victory. "But know that I am going to win."

Jasmine stared up at him. Not for the first time, she wondered if she'd taken on more than she could handle. Maybe Tariq really was the despot he was acting. Perhaps he did consider her a possession.

"I wish to see you, Mina." He turned her with such speed that she would've lost her balance had he not clamped an arm around her waist. His other arm came to lie under her breasts.

When she looked up, she found, to her shock, that they were standing in front of the full-length mirror in the corner. Her hair was exotically red against the white of her nightgown, her pale skin a stark contrast to the darkness of his arms. His big body was curved over hers, his shoulders blocking out the night.

"Tariq, let go," she begged, unable to take the erotic intimacy implied by the reflection. She turned her face to one side, so her cheek pressed against his chest. Her worries about him were buried under the river of need that flooded her body.

"No, Mina. I wish to see you." He nuzzled her neck, brushing aside the strands of her hair in his path. "I have fantasized about this for years."

His rough confession made her tingle from head to toe. It no longer felt wrong to know that his eyes were on the mirror, seeing everything she attempted to hide. It felt completely right, as if she had been born for this moment. Born to be the woman of the Sheik of Zulheil.

"Watch me as I love you." He nipped at the side of her neck, then suckled the spot.

She shook her head in mute refusal. Despite the feeling of

rightness, she was too innocent, too untouched, to easily accept this level of sensual discovery. Tariq kissed his way up her jaw and over her cheek. Her earlobe was a delicate morsel to be sucked into his mouth and savored. He ran his teeth over her skin in a gentle caress. Jasmine shivered and stood on tiptoe in an unconscious attempt to get closer.

"Look in the mirror," he whispered, spreading his fingers across her stomach and under her breasts. "Please, Mina."

His husky "please" broke through her defenses. She turned her head and looked. And met his burning green-eyed gaze. Holding her eyes, he moved the hand under her breasts until he was cupping one full globe. She gasped and gripped the arm at her waist. In response, he squeezed her aching, swollen flesh. It wasn't enough. She needed more.

"Tariq," she moaned, shifting restlessly against him.

"Watch," he ordered.

She watched.

He moved his hand up until his thumb lay near her nipple. Under her wide-eyed gaze, he rubbed his thumb over the throbbing peak once, twice, and again. She was panting for breath. Behind her, she heard his own breathing alter, felt his body harden, muscles and tendons settling into unyielding lines. She cried out when he stopped caressing her, only to sigh and whimper when he repeated the teasing stroking on her other breast. His hands were big, sprinkled with dark hair, and Jasmine ached to feel them everywhere. When he moved, she dropped her hands to her sides.

He left her breasts aroused and hot. His hands moved over her stomach, smoothing their way to her hips. There, he very carefully spread his hands so that his thumbs met in the middle across her navel. She dug her fingers into the rigid muscles of his thighs behind her when she saw the way the action framed the shadowy curls between her legs. He murmured in approval against her ear and rewarded her with another teasing nibble of her sensitive earlobe.

Then he smiled at her in the mirror, a very male, very satisfied smile. Still holding her gaze, he moved his thumbs. The curving arc rubbed the top of her curls. Jasmine tried to shift but his upper arms held her shoulders pinned to his chest. She watched in helpless fascination, her heart thudding in her throat, her knees losing their strength, as he slowly, deliberately pushed his thumbs down and inward.

The sudden pressure on the tiny bundle of nerve endings hidden under the fiery curls made Jasmine scream and bury her face against his chest. He let her recover before repeating the intimate caress again and again, until she was arching into every touch, urging him on. Dazed, she met his gaze. His eyes were hooded and dark, but the flush high on his cheekbones assured her that he was as affected as she was.

"No!" she cried, when he removed his hands.

"Patience, Mina." His breathing was irregular, but his control intact.

Jasmine squirmed in an effort to make him return. Instead, he gripped her gown at her hips and started to gather the soft material into his big hands. She was bare to her thighs before she registered his intent.

"No!" She tried to lift her arms but he squeezed with his biceps, trapping her. Unable to watch as he claimed her so blatantly, she pressed her eyes shut. And felt his lips on her neck, on her temple, on her cheek. He stopped raising the nightgown.

"Mina." It was an invitation into sin. Jasmine couldn't resist. She opened her eyes and watched him bare her to the waist, mesmerized by the rich sensuality of his voice.

"Oh, God." She felt like a complete and utter wanton, standing there unveiled, her legs parted for balance, Tariq a dark masculine shadow behind her.

His thigh muscles moved fluidly under her hands as he changed position. To her shock, she felt one thickly muscled thigh slide between her legs. He began to rub it across her aroused flesh, a gentle abrasion that set her senses reeling. There were no barriers between his heat and her moist warmth. Her hands were free but she no longer wanted to stop him.

"Ride me, Mina." He shored up the gown with one arm

and slid his other one between her legs. Jasmine thought she would lose her mind when she saw his fingers part her curls. He shifted his leg again, inciting her to do what he wanted. Jasmine moaned and, almost without volition, began moving her hips. His fingers stroked her pulsing flesh even as his leg pushed harder and lifted her toes off the floor.

Lost in his touch, she closed her eyes and rode. Desperate for an anchor, she curled her hands around his biceps, but it was too late. She felt the explosion building, and then suddenly, she crashed. It was as if every part of her had broken apart and then reintegrated. Sobbing with her release, she lay against Tariq, trusting him to hold her up.

"Mina, you're beautiful." His voice was reverent.

Jasmine lifted her head and found herself looking at her image in the mirror, her legs spread apart, Tariq's thigh holding her up. Too full of pleasure to blush, she raised her head and met his eyes. "Thank you."

Tariq shuddered, almost undone by her surrender. "I haven't finished yet."

The gown whispered down her lovely legs as he released it. Her fever-bright eyes watched him untie the laces. He took his time, enjoying the culmination of years of erotic dreams. When she moved, he felt the faint shivers that rocked her. Pleased, he flexed his thigh against her sweet heat, knowing it would send shards of pleasure rocketing through her.

"Tariq, don't tease." She tilted her head toward him.

He dropped a kiss on her lips, enchanted by the feminine complaint. "But you are so teasable." He finished with the ribbons and the gown gaped open, baring her breasts. His arousal became almost painful in its intensity, at the sight of a reality that outstripped his every fantasy. Closing one hand around the taut flesh, he squeezed gently.

Mina's eyes drifted shut and she arched into his touch. He nudged her hips, needing her to feel him, to understand this claiming. This branding. He wanted to mark her so deeply that she'd never think of walking away from him again. The urge was primitive and uncivilized, but when it came to this woman, his emotions had never been polite or bland.

Opening her eyes, she smiled at him in the mirror, a smile full of newly realized feminine power, and then began to move her body up and down. The slow dance was an unmerciful tease, but the feel of her was indescribable.

He growled in warning. "Witch."

"Tease," she accused.

He started to fondle her breast again, rubbing her nipple between his fingertips. She was so exquisitely sensitive, it was a temptation he couldn't resist. "Perhaps," he agreed, "but I'm also bigger than you."

Before Jasmine could take another breath, Tariq lifted the gown and tugged it over her head. Her arms came up of their own volition, her mind unable to defy the compulsion. She heard him throw the garment aside at the same time he withdrew his thigh from between hers. Only his arm around her waist kept her upright.

Jasmine pushed aside the hair in her face and gasped at the sight of her naked body displayed so openly for him.

"You are mine, Jasmine."

This time, the blatant possessiveness of his words didn't scare her. No man could touch a woman as tenderly as Tariq was touching her if he only saw her as a possession. Somehow, she had to reach the man she knew existed behind the mask.

She'd hurt Tariq more than she could've imagined when she'd ended their relationship. Now she had to love him so much that he would never doubt her again. Her panther had to trust in her loyalty before he'd allow himself to trust in her heart. And he would, because she had no intention of giving up. She couldn't allow herself to think that there was no hope of winning him back. That was a nightmare she couldn't face.

His eyes met hers in the mirror, daring her to deny him. Instead of answering the silent challenge, she took a deep breath and said, "I want another ride."

Four

Tariq's arm tightened convulsively around her waist and the fire in his eyes blazed out of control. "No, this time *I* will ride." He turned her in his arms and picked her up without effort. "A long, slow ride. You can have another turn later." A hard kiss on her lips sealed the rough promise.

He laid her on the sheets after pushing aside the blanket. For the first time, Jasmine saw him completely naked. He was big. She hadn't thought about just how much bigger than her he was, until that moment.

His eyes met hers and she knew he understood her apprehension. "I won't hurt you, Mina." He moved onto the bed and covered her body with his own. The heavy weight of him was like a full-body caress, a feast for her senses.

"You always call me Mina when you want to get your own way." She spread her thighs for him and wrapped her arms around his neck.

Tariq rewarded her trust by slipping his hands under her waist and cupping her buttocks. "I'll always get my way from now on." His statement was uncompromising, as was the blunt tip of his erection against her.

Then he kissed her, his tongue mimicking the ultimate sensual act. Jasmine knew she was ready; she'd felt herself slick and moist against his thigh. She knew it, but it took his kiss on her breast, his huskily uttered, "I'll take care of you, Mina," to make her believe.

"Now," she whispered.

He gripped her hips and pushed. At the same time, he captured one strawberry-pink nipple into his mouth and suckled. Hard. Jasmine screamed and bucked under the onslaught of feeling, inadvertently easing his way. He surged inside her, tearing through the thin membrane that had protected her innocence. She gasped, her body taut.

"Mina?" He was frozen above her.

She dug her fingernails into his shoulders. "A long, slow ride," she reminded him in a breathless murmur, still adjusting to the feel of his heat inside her.

Three torturously slow strokes later, she was begging him to go faster.

"You are too impatient," he reprimanded her, but his body glistened with sweat and she could feel him trembling with the effort to hold back.

She tightened her legs around him and drew her nails down his back. His eyes flashed as his control fractured and then he slammed into her. Jasmine bit his shoulder when her desire reached a crescendo, and then she felt herself explode for the second time that night. Above her, Tariq went rigid as his own climax roared through him.

His body was heavy when he collapsed on top of her, but she was so exhausted she couldn't move. Instead, she nestled her face in the crook of his neck and fell asleep.

Jasmine awoke sometime in the twilight hours when her stomach growled. Only then did she realize that, as a consequence of her nervousness, she hadn't eaten since she'd left New Zealand. She attempted to shift, and found she couldn't.

One heavy male leg pinned her lower body to the bed and the arm curved possessively under her breasts immobilized her torso. Her stomach growled again.

"Tariq." She turned her head and kissed his neck. Under her lips, his skin was warm and tasted faintly of the desert and the salt and spice of their loving. "Wake up."

He groaned in his sleep and tightened his embrace. Sighing, Jasmine put her hands on his shoulders and shook him.

"You wish for your ride already, Mina?" His sleepy question made her turn bright red. Now that she wasn't in the grip of passion, she couldn't believe her boldness.

She frowned. "I wish for food. I'm starving."

He chuckled and rolled over, taking her with him. She ended up sprawled on his chest. His eyes glinted at her from behind half-closed lids. "What will you give me if I feed you?"

Her stomach growled again. Loudly. "Peace."

This time he laughed, his chest rumbling under her hands. "Ah Mina, you are never what is expected." He gave a long-suffering sigh. "I'll see if I can find you food."

He put her aside with careful hands and slipped out of bed. Jasmine couldn't help watching him. The well-defined muscles of his back bunched as he stood up and bent over to pick up the robe he'd pushed out of her hands.

"Like what you see?" he asked, without turning around.

Jasmine felt herself blush again. "Yes."

He was pleased by her answer. She saw his smile when he turned to walk out, shrugging into the robe.

"Where are you going?"

"There is food in the dining area. I'll bring it to you."

After he left, Jasmine quickly found her rumpled gown and slithered into it. She was sitting cross-legged on top of the blankets, hoping the shadows hid the sheer quality of the gown, when he came back. Not saying anything, Tariq put the tray of food in the center of the bed and lounged on the other side like a lazy panther, watching her eat.

"So, what's my name now?" she asked, once the sharp edge of her appetite had been dulled to something bearable.

"Jasmine al-Huzzein Coleridge-Donovan Zamanat."

Jasmine's eyes widened and her hand stopped midway to her lips. She stopped chewing. "Good grief. What a mouthful! I didn't know that I got to keep my maiden name."

"Zulheil's women have always been cherished." He stretched lazily. "It's why we do not ask them to convert their religion upon marriage. The choice is yours."

The words sent a warm glow through her. Yes, she thought again, there was hope. "So Donovan was your mother's name?"

A flicker of darkness seemed to shadow his eyes, but his response was easy. "You know she was Irish." He plucked a fig off Jasmine's plate and put it into his mouth. For a minute, she just stared at the sensuous shape of his lips, reminded of the things he'd done to her with that clever, clever mouth.

"When we have a child, he or she will have al-Huzzein Coleridge Zamanat as their name. Al-Huzzein Zamanat is the name of the ruling family, but their mother's name is also always carried by the children."

He glanced curiously at her when she didn't reply. She blushed and transferred her attention back to her food. The thought of carrying Tariq's child caused bittersweet pain. She knew she had to tell him her secret…but not now.

"You have her eyes."

"Yes. And…" He paused. When Jasmine looked up, he smiled his dangerous smile. "Some would say I have her temper."

"They're obviously bright people." She picked up a dried apricot and fed it to him. He caught her wrist in a lightning-fast move and licked her fingers clean, like a great big cat lapping at his meal. His eyes never left hers.

"You must miss them." Swallowing, she fought the sensual promise in the air to address something far more important.

He looked away from her, into the shadows. "They are gone. I must lead my people now. I have no time to mourn."

Jasmine hurt for him. Everyone should be given the chance to grieve. Even a sheik. She'd opened her mouth to offer her support when he took the tray of food and put it on the floor. "Enough talking." He tumbled her to the bed.

Tariq did not wish to talk of his parents. The pain of their deaths had been intense. What he'd discovered afterward had almost driven him mad with grief. His beautiful, loving mother had been dying of cancer. His parents had been on the way back from a clinic when the car crashed.

The woman he'd trusted most in the world had kept a secret that had stolen her from him before her death. He'd had so many things to tell her, but because she hadn't had enough faith in him to share her secret, he would never get the chance. And he'd never know if there was something he could've done that would have averted tragedy.

Shaking off the memories, he pressed Jasmine into the mattress, pleased by her instant acceptance. Here, there would be no lies between them. There would be no secrets in the pleasure their bodies found in one another. He shoved aside the errant thought that there couldn't be such passion without emotional consequences, unwilling to concede that this tiny woman, with her gentle smiles and lush sensuality, might have already found a foothold in the lost places of his soul.

"You are sore?"

He could tell that she blushed by the hotness of her skin under his palm. Her heart's ragged beat became even faster.

"No." She hid her face against his neck.

"I won't force you, Mina. Never will I take what is not freely given." He stroked her back and pressed a line of kisses down her throat, luxuriating in her softness. Mina's delicious curves made him want to conquer her feminine secrets with slow, languorous enjoyment.

"Can I force you?"

He was startled for an instant by the suggestive whisper, and then he smiled. "Do you want me so much then, my wife?"

"You know I want you." Those eyes of hers flashed fire

at him, unexpected and delightful. Again he had to acknowledge that this Mina wasn't the same girl who'd almost destroyed him four years ago.

He leaned down and tasted her lower lip. Her teeth scraped
gently over his in return. Yes, he thought, this Mina was no
tame kitten to be ordered to heel. This Mina had claws. Would
she use them to fight him or fight for him?

New excitement flickered through his bones.

Two days later, he walked into a turret room at one end of
their suite, just in time to see Mina raise her arms above her
head and say, "Perfect!"

Surrounded on three sides by clear glass, the room was
bathed in sunshine. As Mina danced across the floor, dust
motes whirled with her, as if excited by her laughter. His
whole body clenched. Buried feelings shook off their bindings.
So easily, she could once again hold his heart in her hands.

Shocked by the knowledge of his susceptibility to a woman
whose loyalty had never belonged to him, he fought off the
tenderness she'd aroused.

"What's perfect?" he asked at last.

Startled, Jasmine froze and met Tariq's dark gaze. His
power and charisma seemed to have increased in the hours
that they'd been apart. "This room," she managed to answer.
"I thought I'd use it for a workroom. Is that okay?"

Tariq moved farther inside. "This is your home, Mina. Do
as you wish."

His generosity gave lie to his harsh words in the car. Jasmine smiled and hugged him. He didn't react, and she drew
away before he could think to push her away. Affection was
something completely different from touching in bed, and
Tariq had given no sign that he wanted anything from her
outside of that sensual arena. The knowledge hurt, but she was
determined to break through the barriers between them.

"Thank you." Walking over to one of the windows, she
found that it looked out into their private garden. "This room
would be perfect for your painting. Where's your studio?"

The vibration of the floor beneath her bare feet warned her of his approach. Seconds later, he put his hands on her shoulders and turned her around. "I am a sheik, Mina. I don't have time for such things."

Jasmine frowned. "But you loved painting." She treasured the painting he'd done for her in New Zealand. It had become a talisman of sorts, keeping her focused on her dream.

"We do not always get to do what we love."

"No," she agreed, shaken by the implacability of his statement. Her Tariq, who'd been gentle enough in his heart to truly love, was now buried under the stoney facade of this sheik. Doubts about her ability to reach him surfaced once again, though she tried to fight them. For a woman who'd never been loved by those who were supposed to treasure her despite her faults, it was a task that required a mix of defiant courage and desperate hope.

Tariq closed his hands around her neck and caressed the sensitive skin with his thumbs, his eyes hooded and mysterious. "We do not have the time for a wedding journey, but I am scheduled to visit one of the desert tribes tomorrow. You will come."

He was giving her no choice, but Jasmine didn't want one. She'd spent four years apart from him. It was enough. "Where are we going?" Her skin felt as if it was on fire.

Tariq rubbed his thumb over one particular spot. "I marked you this morning."

Her hand flew to her throat and touched his hand. "I didn't realize when I chose this blouse."

He looked at her, the green of his eyes altered by emotion to something close to black. "You are mine in every way, Mina."

She didn't know what to say to the possessiveness in his tone. It was a little frightening to be the wife of this dangerous man. Sometimes her Tariq appeared, but mostly, all she saw was this cold, glittering mask.

"Such soft, white skin, my Jasmine." His throaty words made her relax. Tariq's desire she could cope with, but when he retreated behind his shields, she wanted to scream with frustration. "You mark so easily."

"Tariq, what—" she began, surprised when he started to undo the buttons on her scoop-necked blouse.

He ignored her fluttering hands. Eyes wide, Jasmine watched his dark head dip and then felt his mouth on her breast. *Sizzling*. It was the only word to describe the sensation of his lips against her skin. She clutched at his silken hair as he began to suck at the soft flesh. Her body felt like one big flame, his touch the fuel. A minute later, he moved away.

Picking up her hand, he touched one finger to the small red mark on her breast. "See this and know that you are mine."

She stared at him, stunned by the possessive act. Yet she was also aroused beyond comprehension, her body reacting to the primitive maleness of his actions.

"Keep thinking those thoughts." He kissed her once, a kiss calculated to keep her aching. "I will satisfy us both tonight." Then he turned on his heel and strode out.

Jasmine felt her knees begin to buckle. She grabbed the window ledge behind her for support. Unbidden, one hand rose to her breast. He'd deliberately marked her as a gesture of possession, of ownership. She remembered the glittering satisfaction on his face, the harsh lines of his cheekbones, the lush sensuality of his lips, and shivered. Part of it was desire, but the other part was a painful uncertainty. She didn't want to believe that Tariq felt only lust for her, not when he treated her so tenderly at times, but this act of branding had been driven by something darker than love or affection. Something that she instinctively knew could destroy their relationship if she didn't find and confront it.

The next day dawned with skies of crystal clarity and beauty so pure and pristine it made Jasmine's heart ache. Such glory humbled her and yet gave her courage.

They left Zulheina in a limousine for the five-hour journey into the hinterlands of Zulheil. From there, they would have to go by camel to the important, though small, desert holding of Zeina.

"Who are the others following us?" she asked Tariq, after they had pulled out of the palace.

"Three of my inner council are coming." He crooked a finger. Jasmine smiled and moved to sit beside him. He cradled her against his body. Unlike the steely intensity of his passion the night before, today he was relaxed, content to just hold her. "At the end of the road, we'll be met by two guides sent from Zeina to lead us to the outpost."

"It sounds isolated."

"It is the way of our people. We are not like the roaming Bedouin tribes, because we settle and set up cities. But for the most part, our cities are small and isolated."

"Even Zulheina isn't that big, is it?"

Tugging off the tie at the end of her plait, he unraveled her hair. Jasmine laid her head against his chest and basked in his unexpected affection. Just yesterday, she hadn't believed it possible that he'd enjoy this gentle touching.

"No. Abraz is the biggest city, the city we show to the outside world, but Zulheina is the heart of the sheikdom."

"Why is Zeina important?"

He moved his hand to her nape and began to rub his fingers over the sensitive skin in a slow caress. She arched into his touch like a cat. "Ah, Mina, you're a contradiction." His amused words made her tilt her head back to meet his gaze.

"In what way?"

He touched her parted lips with his fingers and said, "So free and uninhibited in my arms and yet such a lady in public. It's a delightful combination."

"Why do I know you're going to add something else?"

"I find I relish stripping away that ladylike facade in my imagination. It's very enjoyable to spend time planning exactly how I will make you cry out."

"Now every time I look at you, I'll think you're thinking that." She blushed.

"You would probably be correct." His laughing eyes

warned her of his intention before he covered her lips with his own.

Jasmine wrapped her arms around his neck and relaxed into the slow and lazy loving. Tariq was in no hurry. Pulling her into his lap, he caressed her breasts with hands that knew every inch of her, and gave her a lesson in the pleasures of kissing. He tasted the inner sweetness of her mouth and nibbled at her lips when she needed to breathe, then returned to tempt her with his tongue, seemingly willing to do this forever. She was the one who got so heated she began to wriggle.

"No more," she gasped, and broke the kiss, aware of the hard ridge of his arousal under her bottom.

His eyes were slumberous, his desire clear, but he pulled down her tunic and settled her beside him on the seat again. "You're right, Mina. I would need hours to finish this."

Flustered and aroused, she scooted to the other side of the car. "Tell me about Zeina before you start your work."

His smile was very male as he gazed at her heaving breasts. "Zeina is one of the major suppliers of Zulheil Rose. For some as yet unknown reason, the gem only exists alongside deposits of oil. It is a strange crystal."

Jasmine whistled. "Talk about double dipping."

"It could be like that, but over centuries, the tribes of Zulheil have set up an interconnecting system that means that not just those people living near such bounty will benefit. For example, the Zulheil Rose leaves Zeina in a condition close to its raw state. It then goes out to two tribes in the north, who train the best artisans in the world."

Jasmine knew Tariq's pride was justified. The artisans of Zulheil were considered magicians. "Wait a second." She frowned in thought. "If the crystal is only found next to deposits of oil, why isn't Zulheina an oil center?"

"Zulheina is odd in more than one sense. Contradictory as it seems, our engineers and geologists insist there is not an ounce of oil in the area," he informed her. "So we think of the palace crystal as a gift from the Gods."

"I can't argue with that. It's so beautiful." She sighed in remembrance. "What's the purpose of this trip?"

"We're a scattered people. I make it a point to visit each tribe at least once a year." He stretched out his long legs, taking up even more of her space. "I'm afraid I must read these reports now, Mina." He gestured to some papers that he'd slipped into one of the pockets lining the limousine doors.

She nodded in acquiescence, thinking over everything he'd said. It was clear that while Tariq didn't yet trust her with his love, he had no qualms about sharing the business of his sheikdom with her. For the first time in her life, she felt a part of something greater, not just an outside observer. With hope renewed in her heart, she plucked a small sketchbook out of her purse and began to design a dress of moonlight and silver.

Tariq looked up from his papers to find Mina's hand flying in graceful strokes across the page. Her face was intense in concentration, her mouth set in a way that suggested something had caught her attention. He was fascinated.

When they'd first met, she'd been a student, but her studies hadn't captured her interest. Today, she was fully absorbed in her thoughts. This was, he realized with a sense of wonder he couldn't fight, the first time he'd truly come face-to-face with the woman his Mina had grown into.

"May I see?" he asked, wanting to learn about this new Jasmine, this woman who threatened to catch him in a net far stronger than the one that had ensnared him four years ago.

Startled blue eyes looked into his, but then a slow smile bloomed. "If you like." At the shy welcome, he moved to sit beside her, his arm along the back of the seat.

He looked over her shoulder. "An evening gown."

"I thought that I'd use material shot with silver."

Her hair was soft against his fingertips as he leaned down to study the clean lines of the drawing. "You're talented. This is lovely."

Her cheeks flushed with color. "Really?"

There was hunger in the need she tried to hide. He recalled

her defensiveness about her designing when he'd first questioned her—the reaction of someone whose dream had never received support. Distanced from the rapier-sharp pain of the past, he began to see a glimmer of the forces that had shaped this woman and her decisions. A kind of furious tenderness for her rose inside him. The urge to punish those who had hurt her while she'd been lost to him was so strong, he had to exercise conscious effort to control it.

"Yes, really. You might find some material to your liking in the shipment that comes from Razarah in the next month." In fact, he'd make sure that bolts were delivered for her perusal. "Tell me about your designs."

Eyes bright, she did. The journey passed in easy companionship that surprised him. Since he'd ascended to the throne, he'd never been free to simply "be" with anyone. Now Mina, with her laughter and her dreams, was tempting him to relax. To play. Did he trust her enough to unbend that much?

Five

"**I**'m scared," Jasmine blurted out.

Tariq turned to face her. "Scared?"

She nodded. "They're so big and…"

To her surprise, he walked over and pulled her into a gentle embrace. "Don't worry, Mina, I'll take care of you."

"Promise?" Her voice was shaky. She hadn't thought through the idea of what a trip on the back of a camel would entail. It had been something vague and slightly exotic.

"What is this?" Tariq moved back, his hands on her shoulders, eyes dark with concern. "You're terrified."

She nodded, miserable. "I can't stand heights and their backs are so high."

"There is no other way to reach the tribe or we'd take it." He cupped her cheeks in his palms.

"It's okay. I can handle it," she lied.

"So brave, Mina." He rubbed his thumb over her quivering lower lip. "The car is still here. You may return home."

Jasmine's head jerked up. He'd been so domineering in his

demand that she accompany him that this concession was a real surprise. "You don't want me to come anymore?"

"I would not have you suffer."

She bit her lower lip. "How long will this trip take?"

Tariq dropped his hands to her waist. "It'll take three days to reach Zeina. With the time I must spend there and the return trip, a week and a half is an optimistic guess."

A week and a half! She couldn't bear to be parted from him for that long. "I'll come. Can I ride with you?"

He nodded. There was approval in the soft kiss he dropped on her lips. "You can snuggle your face against my chest and close your eyes, just like you do in bed."

She blushed. It was true that she liked to sleep with her head on his chest, her arms and legs spread over him, but she hadn't realized that he'd noticed her preference. She raised her hand and stroked his jaw, which was shadowed by his white head covering. "Thank you, Tariq."

"You are welcome, my wife. Come, it is time to go."

Sometimes, Jasmine thought, as Tariq helped her mount the sway-backed creature, her husband could be the most thoughtful of men. He mounted behind her before she could begin to panic. For the ride, both of them were in wide-legged pants and tunics, their heads and necks also covered from the harsh sun.

Her stomach lurched at the camel's first step, but she kept her eyes resolutely forward, determined to conquer this fear if it killed her. The endless desert vista was an unexpected ally, tranquil and beautiful. By the time they stopped for the day, she was watching everything with wide eyes. The camel's rolling gait was a little disconcerting, but as long as she didn't look directly at the ground, no nausea arose. And in truth, her husband's strong grip around her waist almost gave her the confidence to do that as well.

However, she understood that even he couldn't help her with a sore rear. They had stopped at a hidden desert oasis for the night when she discovered just how bad it hurt. After they arrived, she excused herself and walked until she was out of sight of the men. She quickly took care of her needs and then stood in the shadow of a small tree, rubbing her sore behind.

Tariq's low chuckle made her spin around, face flaming. He was standing less than a foot away, his arms crossed over his chest, a wide smile on his aristocratic face.

"What are you doing here?" She dropped her hands and started to walk past him, embarrassed.

He caught her around the waist with one arm and swung her against his hard body. She turned her face away. Tariq nuzzled her neck affectionately. "Don't be angry, Mina. I was worried when you didn't return to camp."

Mollified, and melting from his warm touch, she decided to be honest. "It hurts." For the first time since she'd arrived in this land, she felt ill at ease, a foreigner unused to the ways of these exotic people. She needed Tariq's comfort. What she got was something totally unexpected.

His hands dropped to her bottom and began to massage her aching flesh with soothing strokes. "It will get worse before it gets better. I believe that's a Western saying."

She groaned, too relieved to be embarrassed. His hands felt like magic, but she knew that if he kept going, she'd do something silly like ask him to make love to her. Shoving at his chest, she backed away, her legs shaky.

"We, um…better return or we'll miss dinner." She didn't look him in the eye, afraid of her own hungry desire.

His disappointed sigh was loud in the silence. "You are correct, Mina. Come." He held out his hand. Jasmine slipped her palm into his and they made their way to camp.

Her wicked husband leaned over and said, "I promise to soothe your sore muscles tonight, my Jasmine. I wouldn't have you so aching from riding that I couldn't ride you," just as they reached camp. A blazing blush stole over her.

The other men took one look at her and smiled knowingly. Ignoring them, Jasmine sat down next to Tariq. He sat to her left and a little in front of her, protecting her from the curious looks. Jasmine almost smiled at his possessiveness, but didn't challenge him. Aside from the fact that she was relieved she didn't have to face everyone in her current state, she would never dishonor Tariq in front of his people. In private, she felt free to question him, but deep instinct told her it would be a betrayal to do so publicly.

It wasn't just that Tariq was sheik in a desert land, where men possessively protected their women even as they cherished them. It was him. He was a very private man, a man who met the world wearing a mask. His pride was tied to his inherently private nature.

To his people, Tariq was approachable and kind, but he maintained an aristocratic reserve that was appropriate to his role. However, in New Zealand, he'd utterly frozen out her family, his contempt for their manipulative games completely undetectable. Yet with Jasmine he'd been warm, playful, teasing and, most of all, loving.

Four years later, she understood that only she had seen the man behind the mask. He'd trusted her. Even now he was really himself with her only occasionally—times when he seemed to forget the past. The rest of the time, he wore a mask for her, that of a man who would "own" his woman. It *was* a mask, she told herself. Her Tariq was hidden behind it.

After the evening meal, there was a short discussion in the native language of Zulheil. It was a beautiful language, but one she hadn't yet mastered.

"You were discussing sleeping arrangements?" she asked Tariq, when he turned to her. His eyes were hooded by the edge of his headgear, but she could see the campfire reflected in their depths. Her body began to burn with an inner blaze that was hotter than anything the desert could create.

"Yes. We carry tents with us if you wish to use one."

Jasmine shook her head. "No, I want to see the stars."

He smiled, as if she'd made him proud. "We will sleep away from the rest of the men."

Remembering his promise, she blushed. "Won't that be a problem?"

He raised an aristocratic eyebrow. "No man would let his

woman bed down where other men may look upon her sleeping face.''

''That sounds very...''

''Primitive? Possessive? I am all those things where you are concerned, Mina.''

With the wild desert surrounding them and the night sky sparkling overhead, his words sounded exactly right. He was a warrior into whose keeping she had given her life, and she knew that he would always protect her.

''What, no arguments?'' he asked, when she remained silent.

''How can I argue with a man who has promised me a massage?''

For once, her controlled husband looked disconcerted. It only lasted a moment, but it was enough. The desire between them was mutual, a living, breathing thing. Unlike the loneliness of her love, when he took her in his arms, they were very much partners.

''I think it is time to retire.'' As he spoke, Tariq's eyes glowed with inner fire, not reflected flames.

They left the others soon afterward, carrying their own bedding. Tariq waved off offers of help, saying that if he couldn't make a bed in the desert, he wasn't worthy of being sheik. His men nodded solemnly, pleased with their leader.

He made Jasmine wait while he lay the bedding on top of a thick patch of some springy vegetation that would cushion their bodies from the hard ground. Then he held out his hand. ''There is one thing, Mina.''

''What?''

''Tonight, you cannot make a sound. We are too close to the others.'' He'd already removed his headgear. Now he took hers off and put it aside, before tangling his hands in the heavy fall of her hair. A rough sigh betrayed his pleasure. ''Not a single sound, my Jasmine.''

''Not a single one.'' Her promise was softly whispered.

She didn't make a sound when he stripped her and then himself. She managed to remain silent when he kept his promise to loosen her muscles, his powerful hands tender on her abused flesh. She even bit back her cries when his mouth enclosed her engorged nipples. Then his hand moved between her legs.

Jasmine bit his shoulder. He continued to play with the soft, moist folds between her thighs until she couldn't breathe. She sank her teeth farther into firm muscle in an effort to control her scream. Finally, after tormenting her for what seemed like hours, he lifted her hips and thrust into her in one smooth stroke. This time, she muffled her cries against his neck. He gritted his teeth against his own cry of satisfaction, his face a study in restraint.

They lay with arms and legs tangled until their skin began to chill from the cool night breeze. Tariq rolled off her and sat up to zip the attached sleeping bags closed. When he propped himself beside her, Jasmine saw what she'd done.

"Oh no." She was horrified at the deep, red marks.

"What is it, Mina?" His concern was clear.

"I bit you." She touched the evidence of her crime with her fingertips.

He grinned. "Thank you."

"I'm really sorry."

"I do not mind. There are two more nights we must spend in the desert. Perhaps you will give me another two souvenirs?"

She remained concerned. "Are you sure it doesn't hurt?"

"Why don't you kiss it and see?" he invited.

Jasmine immediately reached over and laved the spot with her tongue and then pressed a tender kiss over it.

"*Now* I hurt," he growled against her ear. The hardness pressing impatiently against her thigh explained why. "But we'll travel far tomorrow. You must have your rest. Turn around and stop tempting me."

Jasmine laughed at how disgruntled he sounded, but she fell asleep in seconds, despite the embers of desire glowing between them. When she wakened, Tariq was already dressed, which was probably just as well. The look in his eyes said that if she'd wakened a few minutes earlier, he'd certainly have delayed the entire party.

"Good morning, Mina."

"Morning." She sat up and rubbed at her eyes.

"I let you rest as long as possible, but we must be away soon if we are to make the next oasis by the time daylight fades." Tariq's deep voice was a caress in itself, full of sensuous memories.

Fighting off her blush, she replied, "I'll be quick. Give me ten minutes."

"Ten minutes." A hard kiss sealed those words.

Jasmine watched him stride away into the lush foliage, her body craving his touch. Hurried along by the cool wind, she shook off the desire that lay heavy upon her senses, and rose. The morning air was crisp, almost chilly, with no hint of the fire and heat that would descend as the sun rose higher. As she completed her toilette, Jasmine was struck by the way her husband reflected the hidden glory of his land.

Tariq could be ice, and he could be fire. Since arriving in Zulheil, she'd experienced both. Four years ago, she'd never seen the ice. Had she known only half the man? Four years ago…four years lost. Suddenly, she was starving for knowledge of Tariq's life in those lost years. The longing was a physical ache inside of her. Tariq had rebuffed her attempts to discuss the past, but she knew that until they did, they'd never truly be at peace.

"Mina! Are you ready?" Tariq's call cut through her unwelcome thoughts. The warmth in it was an arrow to her heart. Despite her hunger to know, she couldn't bear to disrupt their new harmony by bringing up the past.

She parted the branches protecting her from his view. "Are we leaving?" Other than a few bent shoots of grass, nothing revealed that they had camped in this desert haven.

"I would not starve you. Not when I am the cause of the hunger you must be feeling." The rumble of his voice washed over her. She smoothed her pants, inexplicably shy.

Straightening from his leaning position against the trunk of a tree heavy with dark green, glossy foliage, Tariq skated his eyes over her modestly garbed form with a possessiveness she couldn't mistake. Her breath hitched. When he looked up, she thought she might just beg him to take her.

He crooked a finger.

Some feminine instinct protested that arrogant action, even as the needy part of her wanted to run over and say yes, please. Instead, she stuck one hand on her hip and copied the gesture, with a boldness that, around her husband, felt right.

Tariq's smile was a slash of white in the duskiness of his face. To her surprise, he obeyed her command and walked over to stand in front of her, so close that her breasts brushed his chest with every breath she took.

"What would you do with me, my wife?"

Now that she had him where she'd wanted him, she couldn't think of what to say.

Mina's sudden shyness surprised Tariq. He traced a finger down the cool smoothness of her cheek. She ducked her head, but brought her hand up to cover his. He smiled and bent his knees to bring himself to her level. He surprised her with his sudden descent, and that was the only reason he saw the shadows in her eyes.

He rose to his full height, thunder pouring through his veins. She was hiding something. "What is worrying you?"

She jerked her head up. Hair the color of shattered rubies tumbled over his hands. Blue eyes displayed her distress at being found out. "What do you mean? I'm fine."

Her small lie only made him more determined. What was she thinking that she had to hide it from him? Where she was concerned, he'd learned to trust his instincts. Mina called to the part of him that was wild, primitive, untamed, a part that could be dangerous if he didn't keep it leashed. Complete possession of Mina was the payment demanded by the wildness for four years of imprisonment.

"I am your husband. You will not lie. Answer me." He thrust his hands through the fiery silk. The last time she'd hidden her thoughts from him, she'd been convincing herself to walk away. It had almost destroyed him. He didn't think he would survive if she ran from him a second time.

"We'll be late," she protested.

Time was no longer important. "They will wait." His voice was made rough by his knowledge of his vulnerability to her.

"This isn't the place." She put her hands on his chest, as if to push him away.

"You *will* answer me."

The small hands on his chest curled into fists. "You are so arrogant, sometimes I want to scream!"

The explosion almost made him want to smile. Mina's temper delighted him. Only the knowledge that she was hiding something from him curbed the urge. His mother had hidden her illness and it had cost him his chance to say goodbye…and maybe more. Mina's secret could cost him his wife. "I am simply willing to go after what I want."

"So am I." Her voice was fierce. "I came to you."

"And you will stay." He would not give her a choice. "Is this primitive land starting to lose its charms?"

She rolled her eyes, impertinent in her anger. "No, but you're driving me crazy with your questions."

"Answer me and I will ask no more." His logical response made her grit her teeth. Those magnificent eyes flashed lightning at him.

"I'll tell you later."

"Now." He kept her in place with his hands in her hair, clenching thick handfuls of the luminous strands.

She looked away from him. Her body was poised for flight but there was nowhere for her to go. In its blinding starkness, his land was his greatest ally. As he watched, the realization of her weakness dawned on her.

"You're taking advantage of your strength." Her hunted expression accused him.

"I will use every advantage I have." He would not, could not, lose her. She was as vital to him as breathing.

For a second, their eyes met. Silence hung between them, his implacable words almost visible in the air.

"What does it matter what I was thinking?" He knew she was clutching at anything that might offer a reprieve. The hint of victory sharpened his hunter's instincts.

"You belong to me, Mina." This time she'd have no secrets from him. Perhaps, he acknowledged, her youth had made her vulnerable to the pressures she'd been put under four years ago. But if he'd known of those pressures, he would have been ready to fight for her and might not have had his heart ripped to pieces.

Her sigh signaled defeat. "I was thinking of the past."

Some of the chill that had retreated under the fire of their heated conversation returned with a vengeance. "Why do you think of such things?" The past held only pain and betrayal.

"I can't help it. Not when it stands between us." Her expression was earnest, her words passionate.

As Jasmine had feared, the mention of the past blighted the incipient joy of the day. Tariq's smile was only a memory now, this hard-visaged desert warrior the reality. He didn't deny her statement and the silence grew until it pressed heavily upon her. Wary of the stranger he'd become, she lay her hand on his left bicep. The muscle was inflexible.

"Four years, Tariq." Her emotions were naked in her voice. "Four years we were apart, and you refuse to share even a crumb of your life during that time."

His expression grew even darker. "What would you know?"

The question stunned her. She'd been expecting a harsh reprimand or perhaps cold dismissal. For a moment, shock kept her silent, but then words tumbled out of her. "Anything! Everything! Not knowing about those years is like a hole inside me, a part where you're missing."

"You made that choice."

"But now I've made another choice!"

The infinitesimal turning away of his face was his only response.

"Please," she begged.

He released her. Startled, she swayed before regaining her

balance. Stepping back, he regarded her with eyes darkened to the color of ancient greenstone. "I was the subject of an assassination attempt by a terrorist organization on my way back from New Zealand."

"No! Did they…?"

He shook his head in a sharp negative as an answer to the question she couldn't bring herself to ask. "They had no chance." When he returned to his position by the tree, her sense of isolation almost overwhelmed Jasmine.

"Are they still active?"

"No, they were supported by their government, which was overthrown two years ago. The new government is friendly and will sponsor no more such attempts."

She thought that he was trying to soothe her obvious pain. That gave her the courage to continue, even though the ice in his voice was an obvious command to withdraw. She almost expected to see the air fog with her breath.

"But even one!"

That was when he delivered a blow so staggering that he might as well have backhanded her. "They thought me weak and an easy target, because a woman had brought me to my knees."

Jasmine wanted to scream in agony. To have almost lost him…and to finally comprehend that her mission would be a thousand times more difficult than she'd believed. Maybe even impossible. The night before, she'd begun to understand the depths to which her husband's honor and pride were intertwined with his private nature. Today, it was painfully clear that Tariq's pride had been savaged by the reason behind the attempt. His strength as a leader, as a warrior, had been questioned because he'd allowed himself to feel. He would not forgive the woman who had been the cause of the insult.

A call from one of the guides interrupted the heavy silence. Tariq replied without shifting his gaze from her, his eyes dark, impenetrable. The syllables sounded brusque and guttural, as if he, too, were keeping strong emotions in check.

"We must go."

She nodded, numb from shock. Unable to trust herself not to break down, she followed him to the main area. He put food in her hands, and when she didn't move to feed herself, he leaned down and whispered in her ear. "Eat, Mina, or I will put you in my lap and feed you."

She believed him. As quickly as possible, she forced the food down. She had her pride, too.

Tariq carefully picked up Jasmine and placed her on the camel, once she'd bolted down the meal. He could see her fighting the urge to bring up the food, but he was ruthless in his protectiveness. She would need her strength to survive the desert journey. He would not let her mistreat herself.

When he mounted behind her, he made sure not to jostle her. She'd been silent since his revelation about the assassination attempt. He didn't like her stillness. His Mina was fire, life, joy. Yet he knew his harshness had caused her withdrawal. He had spoken to his wife in anger, and now that it had passed, he did not know how to bring her back to him.

"Hold on," he said, as the camel stood up, even though there was no need. His arm was a band around her waist. He would never let her fall, never let her be hurt.

She clutched at his arm, but let go the minute the camel was up. Her white headgear gave her a hiding place and frustrated him. He needed her to talk to him. The discovery made him scowl. A sheik didn't need anyone. A man would be a fool to need a woman who'd proved incapable of loyalty. He'd merely become used to her presence and voice over the past day. It was nothing more than that.

"Will you sulk all day?" He knew he was being unfair, but was unable to stop himself. He wanted her to fight back, wanted her to feel as much as he did, even if it was only anger.

"I'm not sulking." Her response held a hint of her customary fire.

Something he didn't want to acknowledge inside him eased

at her response. She hadn't been beaten or broken. "It's better that you know the truth."

"That you'll never again allow me close to your heart?"

Her blunt question threatened to unsettle him. "Yes. I will not be such an easy target a second time."

"Target?" It was a husky whisper. "This isn't war."

His mouth twisted. "It's worse." After her rejection, he'd barely been able to function. He had loved her more than he loved the endless deserts of his homeland, but it had been the desert wilderness that had helped him heal the wounds she'd inflicted.

"I don't want to fight with you."

Her words calmed him and made him gentle in his response. "You belong to me now, my Jasmine. There's no reason for us to fight. This is forever." He would not trust her with his heart again, but neither would he let her go.

Forever. Jasmine lay her head against Tariq's chest and swallowed her tears. At one time she would've crawled on her hands and knees across broken glass for the promise of forever with Tariq. Now that wasn't enough. Forever with a Tariq who didn't love her and would never love her wasn't enough.

The obstacles in her path had grown to almost insurmountable proportions. Convincing Tariq of her loyalty would not be enough. He might eventually forgive her for not fighting for their love against her family, but she doubted it would be easy. But would he ever forgive the second staggering blow to his warrior's pride?

And what if she caused a third, with the secret that had broken a child's heart?

Panic threatened to choke her. No! No one would know about her illegitimacy! No one would shame her husband. Only her family knew, and they valued their position in society too much to let the truth slip out.

You think your prince would marry a girl who can't even name her father? Keep dreaming, little sister.

Four years ago, Sarah had picked at her most vulnerable spot and then kicked hard. Jasmine still hadn't recovered from the blow, because she knew her sister was right. How could Tariq accept her, much less love her, if even her adoptive parents hadn't been able to?

He wouldn't believe that she'd been so overwhelmed by the marriage ceremony, she'd forgotten the one vital fact that made her the wrong choice to be his wife. As a girl of eighteen, she'd planned to tell him…until Sarah had bluntly thrown the consequences in her face. Believing her sister, Jasmine had kept her hurtful secret, and her family had used it to batter her down when they'd asked her to choose.

"You will speak to me." The rough order jerked her out of her maudlin thoughts. He liked her speaking to him, did he? Yesterday, he'd teased her that she chattered like a magpie.

Allowing a smile to escape, she let hope fill her heart about her ability to inspire love in this complex man. So the fight would be harder. So what? She'd almost died living apart from him. As long as there was the slightest hope, as long as her panther liked to talk to her, as long as he touched her body like he was starving for her, she'd persevere.

Maybe one day he'd trust her enough, love her enough, to accept all of her. Until then, she'd keep the secret she desperately needed to share, the anguish she needed to fight with his love, deep within her. And she'd make up for that one lie by fighting for other truths, however much it hurt.

"Tell me." Her tone was quiet but determined.

"What?"

"Tell me exactly what they tried to do."

"Mina." Tariq's annoyance was clear. "I have said that the past is the past. If you do not wish to fight, we will not speak of this." His hard body moved behind her as he made an adjustment to the reins held negligently in his left hand.

"And I'm supposed to obey your decree without question?" She was unable to let such an arrogant presumption pass.

He was silent for a long moment. "No one challenges the sheik when he has spoken."

"You're my husband."

"Yet you don't act as a submissive wife should."

His tone was so neutral that she almost missed the wry undertone. He was teasing her, no longer cold, as he'd been after the revelation in the oasis. Jasmine decided to continue her quest for the truth, despite his implied forgiveness for the pain she'd reawakened that morning. If she let it go now, Tariq would always refuse to discuss the past. An incredibly strong man, he needed a woman who would challenge him when required, not buckle under to his demands.

"If you wanted submission, you should've gotten a pet." She didn't add that a submissive wife would bore him out of his aristocratic skull within a week.

His arms tightened around her. "No, Mina, I need no pet. Not when I have you to pet."

The wordplay made her blush. "You speak English just fine when you put your mind to it," she noted. "But I'm not going to be distracted."

"No?" Under her breast, his arm suddenly came to life. Muscle flowed and shifted, caressing her without any visible movement.

"No." Her voice was firm, though desire crackled through her like white lightning.

He slid his hand down to press against her stomach. Then, without warning, he said, "We stopped in Bahrain on our return, for diplomatic reasons. On the way from the airport, my car was separated from the cavalcade by two large trucks."

"Hiraz?"

"I was not good company at that time." Tariq's quiet response drove another nail into the bruised flesh of her heart. "Hiraz was riding in the foremost car with two guards. Another two were in the following car."

"You were alone." Instinctively, her hands left the pommel and pressed over his.

"I am never alone, Mina." His words were as close to a complaint as she'd ever heard. Even a sheik, she understood, needed privacy. A man like Tariq would need it more than most. "My driver is always a trained guard."

''What happened next?'' She was caught in the destructive grip of a past that could have physically stolen Tariq from her. As it was, the emotional damage caused by the attack was profound.

He leaned down and moved her headgear aside so he could whisper into her ear. The intimate gesture made her glad that they were riding at the back of the group.

''We took care of them.'' His masculine scent surrounded her, his warmth an experience she didn't want to escape.

''That's all you're going to say?'' she protested, disturbed by the way he seemed to be withdrawing once again.

''There isn't much else. They were religious zealots from a troubled nation who sought to kill me with their bare hands. I disabled three, my driver two.'' He nuzzled her neck, a gesture so achingly familiar that tears threatened. The tone of his voice belonged to an exasperated man tired of a topic, rather than one bent on rebuilding an impenetrable wall.

''And the other guards took care of the rest after breaching the barrier of trucks?'' she guessed.

Tariq drew back from her and pulled the covering close around her face. ''You are too fair,'' he grumbled.

''Maybe I'll tan.'' There was always hope.

His response was a disbelieving snort. ''Enough of this. We will talk of other things.''

She might've argued with him, but he'd already relented a great deal after his initial refusal to speak about his life. Pushing her luck could backfire. ''All right.''

''I don't believe you.'' He sounded so male, so put upon.

''Drat.'' She fell back into the relationship as it had been before she'd learned the awful truth about how Tariq had been targeted for assassination because of his perceived weakness in loving her. She needed to feel his happiness, to find hope in his laughter.

''How are you feeling?'' he asked.

She thought he was referring to their fight. ''This is a beautiful day. It's a day to be happy.''

His chuckle startled her. "I was asking how your sweet bottom was feeling."

She blushed and elbowed him. "Behave." The last traces of frost were long gone. Fire surrounded her. She swallowed tears of bittersweet happiness. There would be no more pain this gorgeous day. She'd pretend that the world was perfect and that the man holding her so carefully, loved her, too.

However, that night, Jasmine couldn't keep pretending that everything was okay. Not when her heart was threatening to break under the strain. "Would it be okay if I retired early?" she asked Tariq. The firelight, which had seemed so romantic the night before, now made her eyes feel dry and achy.

From his protective position slightly in front of her, Tariq glanced over his shoulder. "You do not wish to remain?" His voice had a dark edge that she couldn't decipher.

"I'm tired. This is new for me," she confessed, hiding one truth behind another.

Her husband moved until he was sitting next to her. Then, to her surprise, he pulled her against his seated form. Tariq rarely touched her in public. She hadn't yet found the courage to ask him whether it was because he didn't want to, or because of the circumspection demanded of his position.

"I apologize, Mina. You don't complain, so I forget that this journey must be hard for you." Deep, sensuous, caressing, his words washed over her like soft, welcoming rain.

She nestled her head against his shoulder, finding that some of her inner ache had disappeared. He held her as if she mattered. "Am I expected to stay because I'm your wife?"

His muscled arm firmed around her as he shifted her a tiny bit nearer, eliminating any hint of space between their bodies. "Your intelligence is one of the reasons you are my wife," he murmured. "My people judge those not of our land. It's a flaw in us and yet it's so much a part of Zulheil that it may be our saving grace. We do not trust easily." Jasmine had known that the first moment she'd met him.

"Even though they've accepted you because you are my

chosen wife,'' he continued, gazing down at her upturned face,
''and you'll receive obedience, the amount of respect you receive will be determined by a thousand things, among them
your ability to endure this harsh land.''

She understood what he would never articulate. His honor
was now bound inextricably to hers. It was a fragile link that
could shatter as it had once before, and rip even this shaky
relationship from her grasp. ''I'll stay. Just hold me?'' She
winced at the neediness of her voice.

He answered by touching her cheek with his free hand, his
dark eyes fierce with what she wanted to believe was pride.
Another knot melted inside her. When he looked away, she
watched the play of the firelight on his face. He was at once
beautiful and dangerous. A panther momentarily at rest. A
warrior at home among his people.

Jasmine smiled. Her earlier frustration and pain had faded
to a dull ache. Strangely content now, she stared up at the
jewel-studded night sky, wondering if within those pinpricks
there was a candle to light her way into her husband's heart.

Six

By the time Tariq returned from a last-minute consultation with one of the guides, Mina was curled up and half-asleep. No light from the campfire reached their bed and neither did the voices of the men. He stripped down to the loose pants designed by his ancestors to offer respite from the unrelenting heat of the desert, glad for the small lagoon that had allowed the entire party a chance to bathe.

Memories of watching over his wife while she swam sent familiar need racing through him, but it was clear that Mina was exhausted. Tenderness overwhelmed him. She looked so small and fragile, and yet she made him feel so much. Too much. Heart clenching with emotions he didn't want to accept, he lay down beside her, wrapped her in his arms and let her rest. For a while.

Unfortunately, he didn't get to wake her with slow, sensuous caresses as he'd wanted, because deep in the night she jerked upright beside him, and he could almost smell her fear. He reached up to pull her back into his arms.

"Tariq!" She turned blindly toward him.

"I'm here, Mina." He succeeded in trapping her fluttering hands and held her tight against his body, disturbed by the too-fast thudding of her heart.

"Tariq." This time her voice was a husky whisper, but no less desperate than her first fearful cry. She clutched at his shoulders with small hands.

"Hush. You are safe, my Jasmine." He stroked the curved line of her spine, trying to calm her. When she continued to shiver, he flipped her over onto her back and pressed his body along the length of hers. Some of her tension seemed to seep out of her at the full-body contact. "Mina?"

"They hurt you."

"Who?"

"The men in the trucks. I thought they took you from me."

He hadn't thought that his revelation would have this effect. "I am safe. They did not succeed. You did not lose me." When she looked as if she disagreed, he held her tightly. "You will not worry about these things."

Wrapped in Tariq's strong arms, Jasmine felt her fears start to dissipate. "I'll try. It was probably because I was tired."

"We will not talk of it anymore."

"Wait—" she protested.

He squeezed the breath out of her. "I have decided. You may sulk if you wish, but we will not talk more of it."

"You can't just decide that on your own," she snapped.

"Yes. I can." His voice was neutral, but she heard the steely determination. When he closed his eyes, she knew that any further words would only strengthen his resolve. Sighing, she conceded defeat…for tonight.

Wide-awake, she thought back over her nightmare. Unlike the dream, the real assassins hadn't succeeded in killing him, but they'd broken the connection between her and Tariq, torn the emotional threads. Their taunts had destroyed whatever had been left after she'd walked away.

A man's pride was a fragile thing.

A warrior's pride was his greatest weapon.

A sheik's pride upheld the honor of his people.

She had to learn to deal with the power of all three.

"We're going to finish what we started last night."

"No. I will not have you disturbed." Though Tariq wasn't surprised by Mina's stubbornness, his first duty was to protect her. The memory of how she'd trembled in fear made him hug her against his body as the camel picked its way across the golden sand.

"I'm a big girl. I can handle it."

"No." He would *not* allow her to be hurt.

"Tariq! Don't do that. Don't protect me by keeping me in ignorance." In his arms, her small body was stiff with anger and frustration. "I'm not eighteen anymore."

Her perception about his motives startled him, proving the truth of her words. "Perhaps not," he allowed.

"Then the assassins—"

"You know all there is to know, Mina." This time he acknowledged the quiet pain of the memories. "You *know*."

After a small silence, she leaned back in his embrace. "I'm sorry."

Unable to bear her sorrow, he held her close and told her stories of the desert and his people, and after a long time, she smiled again. And as they rode, he considered her persistence. Four years ago, she would never have challenged him. Since she'd returned to him, she'd never stopped fighting him. Some men would have been dismayed by the change. Tariq was intrigued.

On the morning of the fourth day, they rode into the small industrial city of Zeina. Despite their functional nature, the steel and concrete buildings of the city had been designed with curved edges and flowing lines. Overlaid with the omnipresent sand, the low-rise structures almost blended into the desert. The two-lane highway snaking out of Zeina in the opposite direction from their route showed how oil was moved out of such an isolated spot. To Jasmine's surprise, they continued through the city and a good distance beyond, to where a number of huge, colorful tents sprawled across the desert sand.

"Welcome to Zeina," Tariq whispered against her ear.

"I thought that was Zeina back there." She jerked her head to indicate the city they'd passed.

"It's part of Zeina. This is the heart."

"No houses, just tents," she mused out loud.

"Arin and his people prefer it this way. As they are happy, I have no right to question."

She pondered that for a moment before asking, "I assume many of them work in the industrial section—how do they get there?"

Tariq chuckled. "There are camels for those who prefer the old ways but also several well-hidden all-terrain vehicles."

"Why didn't we travel in those?" She scowled at the thought of the abuse her rear had suffered.

"Some of the areas we passed through are too treacherous to trust even those vehicles. They also cause much damage to the delicate ecosystems of the desert. But, for commuting the distance to the metal city, they are useful," he explained. "Arin's people may be old-fashioned but they are also eminently practical. See the pale blue tents?" He pointed.

"There's quite a few."

"They appear the same as the others, but look closely."

Squinting, she did. "They don't move with the wind! What are they, plastic?"

"A durable type created by our engineers," Tariq confirmed. "Each houses sanitation facilities for use by four closely related families."

Given the dimensions of the tents and the typically small size of Zulheil's families, the allocation appeared generous.

"How ingenious." Jasmine was impressed by the way old and new had been merged so creatively.

"Arin is certainly that."

She met the intriguing Arin minutes later. He was a huge

bear of a man with a short, neatly trimmed beard, but his warm smile took the edge off his menacing appearance.

"Welcome." He waved them both inside his large tent after exchanging greetings. "Please, sit."

"Thank you." Jasmine smiled and sat down on one of the luxuriant cushions arranged around a small table.

"I forbid you to smile at this man, Jasmine."

Jasmine stared at her husband in shock. "Did you just forbid me to smile at the man in whose home we are guests?"

Her subtle reprimand made her husband's lips curve in an inexplicable smile and Arin howl with laughter. She looked from one to the other, belatedly aware that she'd missed something. When Tariq continued to smile with that hint of mischief in his eyes and Arin to howl, she threw up her hands. "You're both mad."

"No, no," Arin answered, his shoulders shaking with mirth. "This one is just afraid of my power over women."

Intrigued, Jasmine turned to Tariq for an explanation, but he just grinned. Shaking her head, she busied herself trying to follow their conversation, which could not be undertaken in English, as their host wasn't fluent enough for the subtleties required.

"My apologies." Arin seemed discomfited by that fact.

"Oh, please don't say that," she said earnestly. "This is your land. I should be the one to learn your language. While I'm learning, it would be better for me to be surrounded by it."

The big man looked relieved. Tariq squeezed her fingers once in silent thanks. Warm, strong, male, his hand represented so much of who he was.

If she concentrated, she could follow the bare bones of their talk. They appeared to be catching up with each other's news but there was an undercurrent of seriousness. The sheik was asking after the health of his people.

As she listened, the changes in Tariq struck her again. When they'd first met, he'd been every inch a royal, but more relaxed, having the support of his parents, a much-loved royal couple. Now the mantle of authority sat on his shoulders alone, and he wore it as if it had been made for him.

He'd always been touched with the promise of greatness. Before her eyes, that promise was being fulfilled.

"Enough," Arin announced at last English. "I am a poor host to keep you so long even before the dust is gone from your clothes." He uncurled his legs, incredibly graceful for such a big man, and began to stand.

"Terrible," Tariq agreed, but his eyes were full of laughter as he followed their host's example. Jasmine's guess that the two were good friends was confirmed by the back-slapping embrace they exchanged, before Arin led them toward the much smaller tent that had been prepared for them. Members of Arin's council had greeted Tariq's advisors upon arrival, and it was likely that they'd all settled in by now.

"Your tent should be larger. I would give you mine but your husband, he is not wanting to be treated like royalty." Arin scowled at Tariq over Jasmine's head. The two men had bracketed her between them as soon as they'd exited. She felt like a shrimp between two very large carnivorous beasts, but one of the beasts was hers and the other appeared friendly.

"If I am in that cavern you call a tent, people will not come to me as willingly as they do if I am in something approximating their own homes." Without breaking his stride, Tariq reached over and tugged Jasmine's headgear around her face, protecting her from the sun. "With you it is different. They have known you their whole lives."

With a sigh, Arin abandoned trying to get Tariq to change his mind. "This—" he waved to a small dun-colored tent "—is to be your home for the next three or four days."

Despite the dull exterior, the interior was beautifully appointed. Colors created bright splendor through the room, in cushions scattered about and gauzy silk hangings decorating the walls. Delighted, Jasmine peeked around the partition dividing the space and discovered a sumptuous sleeping area.

"Thank you. It's beautiful," she exclaimed, bestowing a dazzling smile upon Arin. He looked taken aback.

Tariq scowled. "You will go now," he ordered. "I wish to talk to my wife about the smiles she gives away so easily."

Arin laughed good-naturedly and left, but not before he threw Jasmine a wink. She ran to her husband and tugged his head down for a kiss. He picked her up off her feet to facilitate the soft, urgent caress.

"That is permissible, Mina." He set her down on her feet. "You are welcome to kiss me at any time."

"Gee, thanks." She stepped back to escape him but he was too quick. Tariq held her against him, his hands splayed over her bottom. When she wiggled, he took mercy on her and slid his hands to her waist. "Why did you forbid me to smile at your friend?"

"Because women like him too much. It is very provoking." His complaint was without heat.

"I think he's nice." Her husband's playful mood was a rare treat, one she fully intended to enjoy.

He lifted her up until they were eye to eye. "Really?"

"Mmm." She wrapped her arms and legs around him. "But I think you're the nicest of all."

Tariq's grin was pure male. Her reward for her honesty was a kiss that was so hot, she felt singed.

They ate dinner with Arin and other members of the camp in Arin's huge tent. Jasmine liked being able to watch her sheik among his people. He was magnificent. Charisma flowed from him like a physical substance, bright and clear and utterly seductive. People listened when he spoke, and answered his questions without hesitation, basking in his attention.

"Your accommodations are suitable?" Arin asked.

She had to force herself to look away from her husband, aware that the moment she did so, Tariq glanced at her. His obvious awareness of her, even in the midst of a busy dinner, warmed her to her toes.

"They're lovely. Thank you." She smiled. "I've been forbidden to smile at you because women like you too much."

Arin stroked his neat beard. "It is a curse I must bear. It makes finding a wife difficult."

Jasmine thought she'd misunderstood. "Difficult?"

"Yes." He looked mournful. "How can a man pick one lovely fruit when every day he is confronted with an orchard?"

She clapped a hand over her mouth to muffle her laugh at his outrageousness. No wonder he and Tariq were friends. Right then, her husband tugged at her hand. Though he was talking to someone else, it was an unmistakable sign that he wanted her attention on him. She knew that he wasn't really worried about Arin's affect on women, so his possessiveness puzzled her.

"He is like a child, unwilling to share you," Arin whispered, leaning over. "He is correct in this."

She ignored the last part of that statement and concentrated on the first. It was true. Tariq was unwilling to share her— sometimes. He liked having her interact with his people and make friends such as Mumtaz, so he was no controlling oppressor. However, he seemed to want to keep her close.

What she didn't know was whether he wanted her near because he needed her, or because he didn't trust her out of his sight. She swallowed her hurt at the possibility that it was the latter, and smiled brightly at the woman sitting across from him. Taking that as a sign of encouragement, the woman drew Jasmine into conversation.

"Today, I intend to view several Zulheil Rose mines." Tariq finished his breakfast the next morning and stretched. The power and beauty of his impressive musculature made Jasmine catch her breath. "It will require hard riding, so unfortunately you cannot accompany me."

She scowled in disappointment. "Maybe next time. After we get back home, you have to teach me to ride those beasts."

He smiled at her mock shudder. "I'll do that, Mina. While you are here, you may wish to…I do not know the word, but it would be good if you would walk among the people."

"Oh, you want me to mingle?"

"Yes. Especially with the women. Out here in the desert, a lot of them tend to be shyer than their city counterparts."

"So you want me to talk to them and make sure they're doing okay?"

He nodded. "You are a woman and you are friendly, especially as you continue to smile at everyone." His tone was disgruntled but his expression approving. "Most of the Zeina citizens will try to come to meet us. It is the way we strengthen the bonds that tie our land together. The men tend to wait for me, but the women will feel easier with you."

Jasmine bit her lip in sudden indecision. She felt more than saw Tariq's relaxed body tense.

"You do not wish to do this?"

"Oh, I do. It's just that…do you think I can? I'm just an ordinary woman. Will your people talk to me?" All her life, she'd never been good enough. Sometimes the past threatened to overcome her hard-won self-esteem.

"Ah, Mina." Tariq tugged her into his lap and held her close. "You are my wife and they have already accepted you."

"How do you know?"

"I know. You will trust your husband and do as he bids."

His autocratic command made her want to grin. If he trusted her with this, then he had to have some faith in her. Perhaps it was even the beginning of a deeper kind of trust. The flame of hope inside her, which had been threatening to go out ever since he'd revealed the assassination attempt, started to flicker with fiery life.

"Aye, aye, Captain." She adopted a meek expression that made him laugh and kiss her.

He rode out ten minutes later into the crisp desert morning. After waving him off, Jasmine took a deep breath and began to walk toward the heart of the camp. Within moments, she was surrounded by Zeina's women, surrounded and welcomed.

It was only as dusk began to descend in purple strokes

across the desert that she returned to their quarters. After washing the grit and dust of the day from her body, she dressed in an ankle-length skirt and fitted top in a beautiful shade of gold and lay down on one of the low couches to wait for her husband. Lulled by the soft chatter outside, she closed her eyes, intending only a moment's rest.

Once again, Tariq found Mina asleep. This time he needed to wake her, to satisfy not carnal hunger, but something far more dangerous. "Wake up, my Jasmine." His voice was rough.

"Tariq." With a wide smile she opened her eyes and her arms and tempted him into her embrace. "When did you return?"

"Perhaps forty minutes ago. Now you must awaken so we can eat." Nevertheless, he leaned toward her and let her put her arms around him. Spending the entire day apart from her for the first time since their marriage had brought old pain to the surface—raw, jagged pain that mocked him for pretending he didn't need her. The truth was that he needed her far more than she would ever need him.

"With Arin?"

"No." He smoothed the tangled strands of her hair off her face. "Just me. Tomorrow we'll dine with our people again."

Not wishing to face the emotions she aroused, he started to leave. She held him tight. "Don't go. I missed you."

"Did you, Mina?" He couldn't keep the edge out of his voice. He needed her, but would never again chance entrusting her with that knowledge.

"Yes. I kept looking for you all day." Her eyes were soft, her body warm from sleep.

"Show me how much you missed me, Mina. Show me." He clasped her to him possessively, the wounded beast inside him unsatisfied with less than complete surrender.

He stripped her so quickly that she gasped, but made no protest. He laid her down on the thick rug on the floor, inflamed by the sight of her creamy skin and fiery hair against the scarlet-and-gold material. She was like some pagan fantasy, a dream designed to drive men wild.

Wrapping his hand around her neck, he kissed her, claimed her. He tasted every corner of her mouth while his free hand roamed her body, then covered the soft mound of one breast, making her whimper. Finally breaking the kiss, he bent down to take a tightly beaded nipple into his mouth. He sucked. Hard.

She bucked under him and her hands clenched in his hair. "Please…please…"

The broken sounds urged him on. Nudging apart her legs with his knee, he settled in between them, opening her to him. One hand flat on the rug beside her, he raised his head and looked down at her as he moved his other hand to her stomach and inexorably lower. Sky-blue eyes bled into indigo and lush lips parted in a fractured breath as he found the small nub hidden in her curls.

Though he was careful not to hurt her, this woman of cream and fire, his strokes were firm. Mina clutched at his arms and he could feel pleasure exploding inside her. He stroked harder, leaving her only for the instant it took to lift her right leg and place it over his hip, giving him full access to her secret places.

Her moan when he touched her again wasn't enough. He needed more. He needed Mina's utter and total submission. He needed her to hold nothing back from him. Needed her to need him like he needed her. Needed her to love him so much she would never leave him again.

Reaching lower, he slipped a finger inside her. Her body jerked. Her skin dampened. Then he lowered his head and lightly, carefully, bit the underside of one plump breast. Around his finger, her muscles clenched in an intimate fist so tight he was drenched, surrounded. It was at that moment, as she shoved a fist in her mouth to muffle her cries, that he removed his hand, released himself from his pants and surged into her. Unable to control the spasms overtaking her, she held on to him, biting his shoulder to silence her gasps and moans.

He welcomed the sweet pain. Mina had fallen over the edge

and he could feel it beckoning, but he wouldn't surrender. Not yet. Gripping her hips, he thrust hard. Fast. Deep.

Branding her.

"You're mine, Mina. Only mine." The words were wrenched out of the part of him that raged to claim her for all time.

Only when she lost the battle to muffle her pleasure and her cry rode the night air did he allow himself to fall into the beckoning void.

It was at the final dinner with Arin that Jasmine learned about the relationship between the two men. While Tariq was deep in conversation, Arin answered her questions.

"Tariq spent time in each of the twelve tribes after he turned twelve. This was to teach him about his people."

Jasmine thought that the experience must have been unutterably lonely. He would have been one of them but also, as their future leader, set apart. Her heart ached for the boy he'd been, but she could see the results of his training. Tariq mixed as effortlessly with these desert dwellers as he did with his people in the city.

"He came to Zeina at fifteen and we became friends."

Arin's words were simple, but she understood the depth of that friendship. Her husband didn't bestow his trust lightly. And once that trust had been breached...

"And you've remained friends." She swallowed her sudden apprehension and turned a bright smile on Arin.

The big man nodded. "He is my friend, but he is also my sheik. Make him just your husband, Jasmine, not your sheik."

His advice echoed her thoughts of not so very long ago. She knew that Tariq needed freedom to lay aside the heavy burden of leadership, even if only for a few hours each day. It was easy to say but hard to put into practice, especially where her stubborn husband was concerned. Without warning, he could change, seeing in her the shadows of the past.

A memory of the bittersweet glory of their lovemaking yesterday flickered through her mind. The complex man she'd married, a man even more fascinating than the prince who'd been her first love, would give neither his trust nor his love into her keeping, unless she proved herself worthy. But she refused to quit trying to breach the walls around his heart. She could be just as stubborn as him.

That night, Jasmine sat cross-legged on their silken bedding and watched Tariq undress in the warm glow of the lanterns. He turned and motioned her over with a tilt of his aristocratic head. She rose and walked toward him. Without words being exchanged, she knew what he wanted. She began to help him remove his clothing. His back was golden heat under her light touch, his body beautiful to her.

"You'd make a perfect harem slave," he commented, tongue in cheek.

She bit him on his back for that remark. "I don't think this primitive desert atmosphere is good for you."

He chuckled at her response. She drew back when he was dressed only in loose white pants. To her shock, he held her gaze and pulled them off in one smooth motion. She couldn't move as he threw the last piece of his clothing aside and stalked to her. It wasn't as if she'd never seen him naked, simply that he had never acted with such sexual aggressiveness. Even his furious loving last night hadn't been this... blatant.

He was a sleek, muscled warrior, rippling with strength kept in check for his woman. She knew that Tariq would never physically hurt her, which only made his maleness more compelling. Lips parted with sensual longing, she raised her head to meet his green eyes, shadowed in the dim light from the lanterns.

"You're overdressed for a harem slave," he murmured, and tugged her nightshirt over her head, leaving her naked.

"What about women?" she managed to ask, though her throat felt dry with need and her thoughts were scattered like tangled skeins of thread.

"Hmm?" He nuzzled her neck. It was, she was beginning

to realize, one of his favorite preludes to lovemaking, as well as a gesture of affection.

"Did they have harems?"

He raised his head to meet her laughing eyes. "You wish for a harem, Mina?"

She frowned as if considering it. He squeezed her tightly. "Okay! Okay! I think I can handle only one of you at a time," she stated.

"You will only ever handle me," he said with a masculine growl.

Jasmine smiled and, without stopping to consider her words, said, "Of course. You're the only one I love."

Tariq turned to stone. She wanted to take back her hasty declaration. He wasn't ready; she knew he wasn't ready. But the words had welled up in her heart and escaped before she could control them.

"You do not need to say such things." Under her hands, liquid silk turned to steel and his warm flesh was suddenly searingly cold.

"I mean it. I love you." There was no going back. Throwing away her pride, she gazed at him, silently begging him to believe her.

Tariq's eyes were midnight dark in the lantern light. "You cannot love me."

"How can I make you believe I do?" She ached for the loss of their joy, their laughter, their blindingly beautiful love.

Too late. She was four years too late.

He shook his head, answering her with silence. In the past, his control over his emotions had fooled her into thinking that his feelings didn't run as deep as hers. Only now, when it was too late, did she understand that she'd hurt him more than she could have believed possible. He'd given her his warrior's heart and she'd thrown it away in her ignorance of its value.

How could he possibly believe the truth after such a betrayal? And yet the truth existed. Her love for him was deeper, richer, more intense now. The child-woman who'd first loved him had matured into a woman who loved him so much she sometimes thought she'd die from the sheer intensity.

When he kissed her, she gave herself up to his embrace, swallowing her tears. Tariq played her like a well-tuned musical instrument, drawing every note of pleasure out of her. But he didn't give her his heart. Her warrior didn't trust her not to hurt him again.

Long after he'd fallen asleep, Jasmine lay awake, thinking of the past and how it had indelibly marked her future. Her husband's distrust was like a razor in her chest, making each breath incredibly painful. Even worse was the knowledge that he believed love weakened him.

"…You'll never again allow me close to your heart?"

"Yes. I will not be such an easy target a second time."

The memory of his implacable expression and his determination to never again fall prey to love haunted her. How could she fight her warrior's pride and his distrust in her loyalty at the same time?

Jasmine woke to find Tariq gone. She missed him. Missed his smile, his morning caresses, his body sliding into hers, completing her in a way that she'd never known was possible between a man and a woman. When their bodies were one, it was as if she could see into his soul for one blinding instant. But only sometimes. Last night he'd shut her out, loving her body with exquisite care but giving her nothing more than his physical passion.

She stood up and quickly ran through her toilette when her musings threatened to make her teary. Then she pulled on a long skirt in a soft peach fabric over her naked skin. She felt exposed even in the confines of the tent and wanted to get covered before she worried about underwear. In her rush to dress, she forgot that they were traveling today and she would need to be in pants.

Her fear was justified. She was reaching for a bra when the tent flap opened behind her and a warm breeze touched her back. Apprehensive, she glanced over her bare shoulder.

"Oh." Relief flowed through her.

Tariq raised a dark eyebrow. "You were expecting someone else?" The flap closed behind him, hiding the incipient brightness of the day.

She blushed. No one would dare enter without his express permission. "I just can't get used to the openness of these tents." With a shake of her head, she turned and picked up the bra.

"Leave it." Husky and rough, Tariq's unexpected command startled her into dropping the piece of lace and satin.

The feel of his naked chest against her back startled her even more. He'd been fully dressed when he'd entered, and she'd turned her back on him only a few seconds before. Unlike last night, this morning his hands were impatient, cupping her breasts and teasing her nipples with more heat than expertise, while he kept her trapped in front of him. He was a little rough and most possessive.

She felt a hot rush of liquid heat between her thighs. It was as if Tariq knew. He slipped one hand under her skirt. Continuing to caress her breast with the other hand, he slid a single finger through her curls.

"You are ready." His husky voice held a note of satisfaction, as if he was pleased at her responsiveness.

Before she knew what was happening, he pushed her skirt up her back and bared her buttocks to him. Too needy to be embarrassed, she gripped his thighs when he put both hands around her hips and pulled her onto him, sliding her down so slowly she thought she would go mad.

"Tariq, please, please," she moaned. "Oh, please."

From the way he growled in approval and gave her what she wanted, she knew that he liked her obvious need, liked the way she wriggled on him and urged him to go faster. Out of nowhere, an image of what Tariq had to be seeing as their bodies joined in wild surrender burst into her mind. It was the final erotic stroke. Her climax was thunder and lightning. She knew that she took him with her, his throaty cry mixing with her scream of release.

Afterward, he held her in his lap, their bodies still joined. She tilted her head back against his firm shoulder and tried to get her racing heart to calm down. A long time later, she swallowed and wet her dry lips. "Wow."

Tariq chuckled against her ear and nibbled on the soft flesh of her earlobe. "Not too fast? I hear women like it slow." His tone was pure provocation, daring her to deny the way she'd burned like wildfire in his arms.

She nudged him with an elbow. "You're a horrible tease, but I'm too sated to argue with you."

She heard his smile in his reply. "So this is what I must do to get your complete cooperation. It could become exhausting."

Jasmine laughed. Tariq closed his hands over her breasts in a final sweet caress before he reluctantly pulled away. "We must prepare to leave, my Jasmine. It is time to go home."

Just before they left the tent, she took a deep breath and put her hand on his muscular forearm. Under the white material of his shirt, skin and muscle moved over bone, seducing her with their effortless flow.

He gave her an indulgent smile, still enjoying the aftereffects of their wild mating. "What is it? I promise you we can play when we get home."

His sensually teasing response made her blush. It was as if last night had never happened. She had her husband back. The shields had dropped, but only as far as they had been before her declaration. It wasn't enough. If she let him deny her love, then this half-life would be all she ever had. And she was tired of never being good enough. Tired of never being loved. Perhaps her flaws made her unworthy of love, but until there was no hope, she would try. This time, she wouldn't let anyone, even Tariq, keep her from fighting for their love.

"Your eyes are getting bigger and bigger." He raised one finger and ran it across her lips.

"I meant it. I love you."

His face underwent a sudden change, from open and teasing

to totally reserved. "We must go." He turned away without another word and preceded her outside.

She sucked in a breath of air that felt like a knife blade slicing across her heart. Oh, it hurt so much to have her love not even acknowledged. But her struggle would be worth it if she succeeded in getting back what she'd lost so carelessly in her naiveté.

Tariq waited for Jasmine outside their tent, careful to keep his emotions from showing on his face. It would not do for his people to see their leader in turmoil.

Why did she do this?

Did she truly believe that she could control him with a declaration of love? Words so easily said…promises so easily broken. He'd offered her his very soul four years ago, and she'd thrown it back at him as if it was a worthless token, after promising him forever. Though he would never let her know it, he still hurt from that emotional blow.

Part of him wanted to believe her, whispering that she was no longer the scared girl who'd crumbled under the slightest pressure, but a woman strong enough to fight him at his angriest. However, Tariq refused to listen to that voice. His heart was still raw from her rejection, not yet convinced of the depth of her commitment.

More than once, when she'd thought him occupied, he'd glimpsed shadows in his wife's blue eyes. His pride had stopped him from hounding her, as he had in the desert, but the knowledge ate away at him. Even now, even after he'd told her so much, she kept her secrets, and that he could not forgive. Women's secrets had always caused him pain.

By force of will, he buried that part of him that had become entranced by her. It shocked him just how close he'd come to laying his heart at her feet once again, even when it was clear that she didn't trust him. He wouldn't make that mistake twice. He couldn't. Not when his vulnerability to her ran so deep it had become his greatest weakness.

Seven

The next few days felt as if they'd sprung fully fledged from Jasmine's worst nightmares. Tariq had withdrawn so completely from her that it scared her. No matter what she tried—humor, anger, pleas, protestations of love—none of it reached him. The strength of will implied by such total emotional excision was a huge blow to her fragile confidence. Tariq could apparently cut her out without a thought.

"Tariq, please," she said, in the car on the way back to Zulheina, "talk to me." She was frantic to make him respond.

"What do you wish to talk about?" He looked up from his papers, his eyes holding the mild interest of a stranger.

"Anything! Stop shutting me out!" She was close to tears, which horrified her.

"I do not know what you mean." He bent his head again, dismissing her.

With a cry torn from deep inside, she pulled away the papers and threw them aside. "I won't let you do this to me!"

His eyes flashed green fire as his hand snaked out and

gripped her chin. ''You have forgotten the rules. I no longer follow your demands.'' No anger, no fury, only calm control. Even his touch gentled and then he let her go.

''I love you. Doesn't that mean anything?'' she asked in a broken whisper.

''Thank you for your love.'' He picked up the papers she'd hurled aside, and sorted them. ''I am sure its worth is the same as it was four years ago.''

The subtle, sardonic barb delivered in that smooth, aristocratic voice hit home. ''We're not the same people as we were then. Give us a chance!'' she begged.

He met her gaze with eyes so neutral they were unrecognizable as her panther's. ''I need to read these.''

He'd beaten her. Tariq's anger she could deal with, but she had no defense against this cold, inaccessible stranger. It was clear that he regretted the indulgences he'd allowed her in Zeina, the small things that had caused her guard to slip. She could imagine his thought processes. He probably thought that she believed she could control him now, because he'd allowed her so much, been so open.

Despite that knowledge, she didn't buckle. Tariq was stubborn, but she'd realized that when it came to loving him, she was obstinate beyond belief.

Their first night back, she was tempted to sleep in her own room, hurting and unsure of her welcome. Instead, she brushed her hair in front of Tariq's mirror and lay down in his bed. And when he reached for her, she went to him. In this place, they connected. Their loving was always wild, always passionate. It gave her hope, because how could he touch her like that, how could he whisper, ''You're mine, Mina. Mine!'' as he moved inside her, if only lust was involved?

A week later, Jasmine pinned some silver cloth in place and picked up her scissors.

''I wish to talk to you, my wife.''

Startled by the deep rumble of Tariq's voice, she dropped the pins she'd been holding in her mouth. ''Don't sneak up on me like that!'' She put one hand on her T-shirt, above her heart. ''And stop looming.''

He frowned, and she knew he was about to remind her that he gave the orders around here. Since their return from Zeina, he'd been more autocratic than usual, and colder. It was hard to battle this warrior every day, but his anger strengthened her resolve. Anger this powerful had to spring from deep emotion.

And, she realized, she was willing to fight the warrior because he was a part of the man she loved. The ice that tempered the fire.

Mentally rolling her eyes, she raised her arms and smiled in invitation. Loving him was the only way she knew to prove that she'd changed. For a moment, she thought that he would refuse, and her heart clenched in anticipation of another bruise. But then he came down on his haunches beside her.

She wrapped her arms around his neck and kissed him. He let her be the aggressor, remaining quiescent in her arms, but Jasmine couldn't forget the power humming just under the surface. He could have taken over at any second, but he let her control the kiss, seemingly content to taste her.

When she drew back, he removed her hands and clasped them between his own. ''I am going to Paris for the week.'' Any fire that her kiss might have aroused was carefully hidden, if it existed at all.

''What?'' She couldn't conceal her surprise. Her hands curled into fists in his grasp. ''When?''

''Within the hour.''

She blinked. ''Why didn't you tell me sooner?''

His jaw firmed. ''I have no need to tell you such things.''

''I'm your wife!''

''Yes. And you will stay in your place.''

The unexpected verbal reprimand hit her like a slap. She bent her head and took a deep breath. ''You know some of the French designers are putting on shows this week. If you'd told me earlier, I could've gone with you.'' She'd come to expect his need for control, could even understand it, but he'd never treated her so harshly, as if he cared nothing for her feelings. She hadn't known that he regretted what had happened in Zeina that much.

He released her hands and gripped her chin between his thumb and forefinger, forcing her to face him. "No, Jasmine. You cannot leave Zulheil."

She frowned. "You don't trust me, do you? What do you expect me to do—run away at the first available opportunity?"

"I may have been a fool once, but you will not make me one twice," he nearly growled.

"I came and stayed of my own free will. I won't run."

"You did not know what you faced when you came." His features were expressionless as he brushed aside her words. "I am not wrapped around your little finger, as you no doubt expected, and I do not intend to be. Because you know this, you will wish to escape. I do not intend to lose you."

She shook her head in denial, but he didn't release her. "I love you," she repeated firmly. "Don't you know what that means?"

"It means that you can turn your back and walk away at any time." Rapier sharp, his jabs made her bleed. But she still wasn't beaten.

"How long are you going to act this way?" she asked him in desperation. "How long are you going to punish me? When is your revenge going to be complete?"

His green eyes had darkened to the color of the deepest sea. "I do not do this to punish you. To want to take revenge, I would have to feel something for you beyond lust, which I do not. You are a possession, prized but not irreplaceable."

She felt the color leave her face. She couldn't speak. Her heart felt as if it was bleeding. In a desperate attempt to hide her grief, she bit the insides of her cheeks hard enough to taste blood, and waited for him to finish.

"I will be involved in matters of state. Hiraz knows how to get in touch with me."

She remained silent, barely able to hear him through the painful buzzing in her ears. When he bent his head and placed a possessive kiss on her lips, she accepted it dully, too stunned to respond. Tariq seemed to take her reaction as subtle defiance because he moved his hand to her hair and tangled his fingers in the long ponytail, gripping her head.

''You will not deny me,'' he growled against her lips. Because he knew her every sensual weakness, he was right. She couldn't deny him. Not when she'd been starving for him for so long.

When he drew back, cold satisfaction gleamed in his eyes. ''I can make you pant for me anytime I wish, Jasmine, so do not try and manipulate me with your body.''

The sensual fires he'd aroused were doused instantly by his taunt. Thankfully, he didn't continue the lesson.

''I will be leaving in forty minutes.'' With that, he rose and strode out the door of her workroom.

Jasmine didn't know how long she sat there, unable to function. She felt as if he'd ripped out her heart and then laughed at her agony. She hurt too much to feel the pain. When she finally rose and made her way to the wide glass doors that led out to a balcony overlooking the main gardens, it was to see Tariq walking to a royal limousine.

He was dressed in a black suit, his tie the vivid green of his eyes, his beautiful hair brushed back. She saw him stop and look up at the balcony. Quickly, she stumbled back into the room. From this far, she couldn't make out the expression on his face, but she knew he hadn't seen her. Then he stepped inside and the car drove off.

It was as if his departure released the paralysis that had protected her from her own anguished emotions. Suddenly close to an emotional breakdown, she scurried through the corridors, praying she wouldn't meet anyone along the way. Once safely behind the locked doors of the exquisite room that was her own, she walked out into the private garden and hid under the spreading tree with the blue-white flowers. The branches were so heavy with blooms that they almost touched the ground, providing her with a scented cave of darkness in which to let go of her torment.

Her sobs came from somewhere deep inside, wrenched out

of her body with such force that she didn't have breath enough
to make a sound. She was destroyed by the sudden insight that
she'd been fooling herself. She'd believed that she could love
Tariq enough to make him love her, a girl who'd never been
loved. She had allowed him every liberty, going so far as to
tie herself to him for life. She'd given him her body and her
soul, keeping nothing back.

And now he'd rejected her gift in the cruelest of ways. She
was nothing but a possession to him, prized but not irreplaceable. He felt nothing but lust for her. Lust! Her illusions of
time healing the wounds of the past shattered under the realization that his actions weren't born out of pain. He just didn't
care if he hurt her.

Had he married her only to humble her? Crush her?

She curled into a ball at the base of the tree and wrapped
her arms around her shaking body, trying to breathe through
the pain that lay like a rock in her throat. Dusk fell outside
but she didn't notice. She'd cried all the tears she had inside,
but her pain was so great she couldn't move.

Freed, the demons that she'd drowned in tears descended
upon her, wanting their pound of flesh. In Tariq's land, in
Tariq's arms, she'd almost managed to forget the lack in her.
The missing part that made her incapable of being loved. Suddenly, the memories of that terrible day in her childhood when
she'd understood the truth flooded over her.

*"Does it bother you that you demanded half of Mary's in-
heritance before you'd adopt Jasmine?"* Aunt Ella had asked
the woman Jasmine had thought was her mother. *"After all,
Mary is our baby sister."*

*"No. She should've known better than to get pregnant by
some stranger in a bar. I don't know what possessed her to
have the child."* The sound of ice cubes hitting crystal had
penetrated the library door. *"We aren't some charity. How
else were Jasmine's expenses going to be covered?"*

"You got a lot more than that," Ella had persisted.

"Mary's inheritance from Grandpa was twice the size of ours."

"I think of it as adequate compensation for having to accept bad blood into my family. Lord only knows what kind of a loser Jasmine's father was. Mary was so drunk, she couldn't even remember his name."

Later, when Jasmine had forced herself to ask, Aunt Ella had taken pity on her and told her about Mary. Apparently, in order to avoid any hint of scandal, Mary had moved to America after Jasmine's birth. She'd never returned. The people who'd raised Jasmine, Mary's older sister, Lucille, and her husband, James, had already had two children, Michael and Sarah, and had been unwilling to take on another, until they'd been given a financial incentive. Yet they'd gone on to have another child of their own—a beloved younger son named Mathew.

That day, Jasmine had been slapped in the face with the fact that any care she'd ever known had been bought and paid for. Searching for someone to love her, she'd written to Mary, saying hello. The response had arrived on her thirteenth birthday, a cool request to make no further contact because Mary had no wish to be associated with a past "indiscretion."

An indiscretion. That's all Jasmine was to her birth mother. And to her adoptive mother she was bad blood. Neither Mary nor Lucille had been able to love her. Today, she was forced to accept that the lack hadn't magically disappeared. She was still unloved. Still unwanted.

The next day, Jasmine decided there was nothing to be gained by crying over something she couldn't change. Despite the hurt that existed inside her like a living, breathing creature, she forced herself into her workroom and picked up the scissors she'd dropped the day before.

She had to do something until she figured out how to handle the situation with Tariq, the man whom she'd married in a blind haze of love. Perhaps she'd made the biggest mistake of her life, but she didn't want to think about that now. Neither did she want to think about the way her old fears and insecurities had tormented her last night.

An hour into her work, she heard a telephone ring, but ignored it. There was a knock on her door a minute later.

"Madam?"

She looked up to find one of the palace staff at the door. "Yes, Shazana?"

"Sheik Zamanat wishes to speak with you."

Jasmine's throat locked. About to ask Shazana to tell Tariq that she was busy, she recognized the possible consequences of asking a loyal staff member to lie, and nodded.

"Please transfer the call to this phone." She indicated the one near the door of the turret.

Shazana nodded and left. The phone rang seconds later. Jasmine stood up and walked over. She picked up the receiver…then hung up. Heart thudding, she hurried down the hallway, into her bedroom and out into the garden. The phone rang again just as she escaped. She hid under her tree.

It was cowardly to hide from Tariq but she couldn't bear to talk to him, couldn't bear to hear the voice that she'd dreamed about for years rip her to pieces with the painful truth about her inadequacy. Last night, she'd believed that all her illusions had been destroyed, but today she realized she couldn't face the total loss of hope. Not yet. Not yet.

Perhaps an hour later, she emerged and made her way back to her workroom. There was a message on the table by the phone. She picked it up with shaking hands. It instructed her to call Tariq at a given number.

"Go to hell!" She crunched the note into a ball and threw it into the wastebasket, then began to work on the top she was making. Her movements were jerky and uncoordinated, as for the first time, anger began to simmer under the hurt and sorrow. So Sheik Zamanat expected her to come to heel when he hollered? She almost stabbed the material with her scissors.

He was about to learn that his wife was not some toy he could throw aside and pick up whenever he felt like it.

Tariq hung up the phone for the fourth time. He was annoyed by his wife's subtle rebellion, but another, more dangerous emotion threatened. That emotion would not let him forget the naked pain in Mina's eyes when he'd last spoken to her.

After so long, the anger and hurt he'd ruthlessly controlled for years had shattered its bonds and lashed out. When Mina had voiced her love, he'd felt as if she'd torn open wounds that had barely begun to heal. The almost unbearable pain had sprung from a need that he didn't want to accept. It had caused him to say things he shouldn't have.

Guilt was not something he was familiar with, but pangs of it had been stabbing him since the moment Mina hadn't appeared on the balcony to bid him goodbye. His sense of loss had shaken him. He felt as if he'd damaged something fragile between them. Only angry pride had kept him from returning to her.

But Mina didn't hold grudges. Once he spoke to her, she would return to normal. And the next time he picked up that phone, he *would* talk to her.

Jasmine felt as if she was getting ready for a knock-down, drag-out fight. She'd ignored Tariq for two days. At first, it had been blind instinct, an attempt to save herself from rejection. She'd had enough of that in her lifetime. Later, when she'd calmed down, she'd realized that she needed some time and distance to sort out her feelings. Tariq had given her a rude shock, waking her up forever to the fact that the man she loved was not the man she'd married.

Did she love this Tariq?

Her mind wasn't completely made up, but her anger refused to be ignored any longer. This time, Tariq would get an answer to his call. A call that came as soon as dawn was breaking over Zulheil. She picked up the phone on the second ring.

"Prized possession speaking." It slipped out without thought. She was horrified, but just a little proud of herself.

There was complete and utter silence on the other end of the phone. "I am not amused, Jasmine," he said finally.

"Well, since I'm not a comedienne, my ego isn't too badly wounded." Sitting in bed, her legs hanging off the edge, she felt the simmering anger start to bubble. "Did you have anything to say or did you just ring to remind me of my place?" Where had that come from?

"You are being obstinate."

"Yup."

"What did you expect when you returned?" A thread of anger crept into his so far calm tone. "That nothing would have changed? That I would lay my trust in your lap?"

"No. I expected you to have forgotten me." It was a cruel truth. "But you didn't. You took me and you married me, giving me a place in your life. How dare you now treat me like…like an object? Like something to scrape off the bottom of your royal shoe? How dare you?" Tears threatened, riding the crest of her anger.

"Never have I treated you as such!" His response was a harsh reproof.

"Yes, you have. And you know what? I don't want to talk to a man who treats me like that. I could almost hate you. Don't call me anymore. Maybe by the time you get home I'll have calmed down. Right now, I have nothing for you. Nothing!" It was the raw pain of her emotions speaking.

"We will talk when I return." His voice held a note she'd never before heard, a note she couldn't understand.

Jasmine hung up the phone with shaking hands, surprised by her own outburst. She'd planned belligerence, but had ended up ripping apart the shields protecting her heart. She hurt. And yet it felt cleansing. She *was* worth more than this treatment. She might not be loved but she was worthy of respect.

Something her husband might never give her.

I could almost hate you.

Tariq stared out at the cobbled streets of Paris, Jasmine's words ringing in his head. He was used to being adored by her, being the center of her attention, as he'd been since their first meeting. He'd never considered being with a Jasmine who didn't treat him that way.

He didn't like the sensation. Not when his need for her ran so deep that he missed her every moment she wasn't by his side. He'd only survived the four years without her by working night and day, striving for mindless exhaustion. Her laughter and affection since her return had been a balm to the hunger inside him. Now she was furious with him.

He'd underestimated the woman she'd become. A woman who apparently felt things more deeply and wildly than he'd given her credit for. She'd always had quiet feminine courage, but this was the first time she'd dared to rebuke him for his actions with such blunt honesty. He finally listened to the inner voices he'd been ignoring, accepting that she'd changed dramatically from the Jasmine he'd known.

That Jasmine would never have hated him.

That Jasmine had also walked away from him.

If he opened his heart just a little, what would this Jasmine do? Would she treat him with the same disregard she'd shown four years ago or…? The possibilities were as intriguing and as tempting as the evocative scents borne on the Paris winds.

But first, he'd have to win Mina back. She was his. She wasn't allowed to hate him.

Eight

"**W**hat do you mean, he's in the courtyard?" Jasmine cried, shoving her hands through her tumbled hair.

Mumtaz shrugged her delicate shoulders. "I persuaded Hiraz to delay him so I could warn you."

"But it's Friday night. He wasn't supposed to be back until Monday!"

Heavy footsteps sounded in the hallway. Mumtaz's eyes widened. "I must go. I wish you luck." She slipped out the door. Jasmine heard her say something to Tariq.

With a muted cry of frustration, Jasmine secured the azure silk robe around her waist. It was too late to change. She didn't want to greet Tariq wearing a robe that hit her midthigh, with her hair loose around her shoulders, but the doorknob was turning. Quickly, she settled onto the stool in front of her dressing table and picked up her brush. At least this way, if her legs collapsed, he wouldn't know.

She heard Tariq enter the room and close the door. Her fingers tightened convulsively around the carved wooden handle of the brush, but she continued the smooth, full-length strokes, ignoring his presence. She felt him move until he was standing behind her. He leaned forward and put both hands on her dressing table, one on either side of her, effectively caging her with his body. She kept brushing her hair, though she couldn't feel her fingers anymore because they were shaking so hard. She didn't look in the mirror, avoiding the trap of green fire that awaited her.

"How's your throat infection?" He reminded her of one of her earlier excuses, not referring to the last painful call.

"Much better."

"I can hear that. And you're feeling well?"

"Yes." She tried to avoid touching her head to his chest. Every time she moved an inch away, he leaned closer, until she was on the edge of her stool with nowhere to go.

"Good. I was worried, as you seemed to be sleeping so much when I called." Though his tone was calm, she knew he had to be furious. He wasn't a man used to being reprimanded.

And she wasn't ready to face his anger. Despite her bravado, she didn't hate Tariq. Her feelings for him were raw and undefined, but they didn't come close to hate, and their depth and promise scared her. What if she began to love him even more deeply than she had all these years?

The heat of his body seemed to surround her. She wondered if he'd subtly moved. It was becoming difficult to continue to brush her hair, because with every stroke, she touched him. She chanced a peek at his arms and saw that he'd lessened the gap between them. He was wearing a blue shirt, his jacket discarded.

He reached out, took the brush from her nerveless fingers and put it on the dresser. Then he tucked her hair behind her ears, baring her face. She froze as he stroked the knuckles of one hand down her cheek in a simple but powerful caress, reminding her of the times he'd done that after they'd made love. She curled her fingers into fists and gritted her teeth against the response he could call forth so easily. The memory of his parting gibe helped, but it wouldn't hold up forever against this gentle persuasion.

"Will you also refuse to talk to me now that I am home?" He continued the lazy caress.

"I'm talking to you right now." She was overjoyed when her voice didn't break.

"No. You are answering my questions and hiding yourself from me."

She didn't say anything.

"You are very angry with me, my Jasmine?" The husky timbre of his voice was close to her ear, his body almost totally enclosing her. "You have not calmed down?"

"I'm not angry." Her heart thudded hard against her ribs. The anger had long since burned out, leaving behind a residue of hurt so deep she felt ravaged.

He kissed the lobe of her ear. A shiver raced through her. She couldn't disguise the instinctive reaction, but neither did she do anything else.

"Ah, Mina, you cannot lie. Come, look at me. Welcome your husband home."

His words were an unwanted echo of his commands before he'd left. "Do you wish to have sex? If you'll move, I'll get on the bed." Dark and violent emotions rose in her throat, daring her to release them. She stifled the urge, refusing to let Tariq see just how badly he'd hurt her when he'd brought her deepest fear to the surface and given it form.

His body turned to stone around her. She could feel his muscles tensing as if to strike. He drew back so fast that she nearly fell off the stool, unbalanced. She'd barely got herself grounded when he lifted her and stood her in front of him. In bare feet, she only came halfway up his chest. Startled, she almost met his eyes but managed to fix her gaze on his shoulders.

"Mina, do not do this. You know you will turn into liquid fire in my arms." He curved one hand over her hip and used the other to cup her cheek, but didn't force her to look up.

"Yes, I know you can make me *pant* at any time." She

swallowed the lump in her throat as she repeated his taunt. A taunt so true it made her cry inside. If he touched her much longer with those sensitive fingers, she'd shatter like fine crystal. Something wild and needy in her recognized his touch and wouldn't let her pull away. "I'm not going to fight you."

He growled at her response and pulled her into a bruising embrace, holding her head against his chest. Jasmine had to fight every instinct she possessed not to respond. Her hunger for him was a clawing being inside her. She reminded herself that she was prized but not irreplaceable. *Not irreplaceable.* He felt only momentary lust when he touched her. When she remained stiff, arms at her sides, he released her.

"Go to bed, Jasmine." He sounded tired and defeated. Leaving her standing in the center of the bedroom, he pushed through the connecting door and into his room.

The door shut with a quiet click.

Out of nowhere, exhaustion slammed into Jasmine. Dreading this confrontation, she'd barely slept the past five nights. Still wearing the silk robe, she crawled under the blankets. However, a sense of loss kept nudging her awake. She knew it was a lie. She'd never had anything to lose. Still, she wanted to go to her husband and hold him…soothe him.

"No." No, she wouldn't give in to the need, when he clearly saw nothing wrong with his treatment of her. Respect, she repeated to herself. She was worthy of respect.

Tariq threw his balled-up shirt across the room. She'd denied him! He'd never expected that from Jasmine. He had relied on her generous nature to forgive him. Time and distance, and Jasmine's passionate anger, had made him regret his cruel words. That day in her solar, he'd allowed the wounded beast inside him to speak, full of years of pent-up anger and pain. It would have been better to keep that uncontrollable part of himself locked up.

He'd been feeling instead of thinking, and the words that had slipped out had been weapons aimed at his wife. More than that, they'd been untrue. He had four years of midnight awakenings to attest to the fact that she was irreplaceable.

What if the damage was irreversible? What if Mina did hate him? Her body had been so stiff in his embrace, her lips so silent. She'd been like a small creature frozen in front of a predator. The painful image forced him to accept that what he'd felt from Jasmine hadn't been anger or a need for revenge, but...hurt. His temper vanished in the face of that truth. He had hurt his wife, his Mina. There was no satisfaction in that knowledge, only disgust at himself. She was his to protect. Even from himself.

For the first time in an eternity, Tariq was uncertain about his next act. A sheik could rarely indulge in indecision, but it appeared that a husband had plenty of opportunity to do so. He knew he'd acted badly, but he wasn't a man accustomed to asking for forgiveness. With a sound akin to a growl, he stalked into the shower, his mind on the small woman with big blue eyes next door.

Familiar hands, rough but gentle, stroked the naked line of her spine. Jasmine frowned, sure that she'd been clothed before sleep, but in this dream, skin touched skin. A kiss on her nape, on each vertebra, possessive hands grasping her hips... She moaned and turned onto her back, welcoming her lover. When he pressed his lips to her breasts, she arched into him. Waking thoughts merged with hazy dreams as her fingers tangled in thick silky hair. A beard-roughened jaw angled across her breast. She shivered and the spot was immediately kissed.

''Tariq,'' she whispered, awake and aware. It was too late to stop her response. Her whole body was open in invitation. Jasmine sighed and gave in to the inevitable. Whatever he said, whatever he did, he was hers. How could she possibly deny him when he touched her as if she was precious?

When he kissed her, she returned his kiss joyously, unable to hide how much she'd missed him. He shuddered against her and broke away to drop kisses across her breasts. Under her fingers, his shoulder muscles bunched as he moved down her body, dropping a line of kisses across her stomach and flicking his tongue over the indentation of her navel.

Shivers racked her body as he found an unexpectedly sensitive spot. Her reaction made him repeat the quick caress. Her stomach muscles clenched and her hips jerked upward without conscious control. Pressed so close, she could feel his heartbeat in the pulse of his body.

She parted her thighs for him without prompting, but he didn't rise to possess her. He lifted her left leg and placed it over his shoulder. Her sensitive skin burned from the heat of his body. Then he rubbed his rough jaw across the tender skin on the insides of her thighs.

She gasped. "Tariq, please."

He soothed the roughness with his tongue, sending her nerves into further disarray. Then he repeated the whole process with her right leg. Just when she thought that she could feel no more pleasure, he dipped his head and bestowed the most intimate kiss of all upon her.

She screamed and would've squirmed away, but his hold on her hips kept her in place as he slowly, and with great care, introduced her to this shatteringly intimate form of loving. His only aim was her pleasure.

With the tiny slice of her brain that was functioning, she knew this was Tariq's apology. Her warrior was adoring her body, cherishing her response. He couldn't say the words, but he was showing her that she was more than an object to satisfy his lust. How much more, she didn't know, but even the depth of her hurt couldn't survive against this kind of tenderness.

She clutched handfuls of the sheets and gave herself up to his caresses. Once more, she gave her heart and soul to Tariq, her vows to keep him at bay disintegrating into dust. She felt the change in him immediately. His intense, concentrated caressing continued, but his shoulders were no longer so tense under her thighs, and his hands were anchors rather than vices forcing her to stay in place. And then she couldn't think. She found the kind of freedom that she could only find in his arms and splintered on the wings of pleasure. He held her until the tremors subsided and then gently entered her, as if unsure of his welcome.

Tears pricked her eyes at his hesitation. He wasn't acting the autocratic despot now. The silent question delivered the final blow to any lingering hurt. She deliberately clenched her inner muscles and held him prisoner, telling him without words that he was wanted, needed, loved. At the same time, she curled her arms around him and dropped kisses across his shoulders. With a groan, he began to move.

"Welcome home," she whispered, just before she crested the highest pinnacle of desire for a second time that night.

A long while later, she gathered enough confidence to ask, "Why did you return early?"

Tariq spooned her deeper against him and dropped a kiss on the curve of her shoulder where it met her neck. "The trade agreement was completed earlier than expected."

"Did you…" She began to ask him about the agreement, then stopped, unwilling to be rebuffed. He'd loved her with fire, but she was afraid that she'd be waking up beside the cool, reserved stranger he'd become after Zeina.

"What, Mina?"

"Nothing."

He was silent for a while and then said, "Zulheil now has a contract with several Western states that will allow our artistic products to cross their borders without duty."

She took the olive branch, prepared to meet him halfway. "Why artistic products?"

"Zulheil's jewelry and other artistic products are highly prized. They are our third biggest export. The agreement goes both ways." He chuckled, warming her heart. "They think their goods will flood our markets, but they're wrong."

"How do you know that?"

"Because, Mina—" he squeezed her with unexpected playfulness "—we have had such an agreement with the United States for years."

"Really? But there's no mass-market stuff in your streets." She snuggled into him, her head pillowed on his arm.

"My people are used to the best handcrafted goods. The riches of the land are shared by all. The cheap things they send are never bought."

"You're snobs."

Her husband shrugged. "But we are rich enough to be so."

His unrepentant reply made her laugh. She couldn't temper her responses to him when he let his shields fall. "So you're getting the best of this bargain? Why don't they know about the experience of the Americans?"

"Nobody likes to admit their mistakes. What would it look like if the world's biggest power had been…I have lost the word," he paused, waiting for her.

"Conned?" she suggested cheekily.

"Yes. It would not look good for them if they were seen to have been *conned* by a tiny sheikdom from the desert. A poor, primitive people."

She laughed so hard that she cried. "Primitive!"

When she'd stopped giggling, Tariq bit her lightly on her shoulder to catch her attention. She turned into his arms, aware that she'd capitulated too easily, without waiting for words of apology to banish her heartache. But she'd always known that Tariq would never humble himself in such a blatant fashion. He was too much the desert warrior for that. For now, his incredibly tender loving was enough.

It was a start.

Early the next morning, Jasmine sat on the edge of her Zulheil Rose fountain, listening to the cool splash of the water and the quiet sounds of the birds. Kept awake by her newly reinvigorated demons, she'd made the decision to leave Tariq sprawled in bed, and face them. Face them and defeat them.

First, she accepted that she'd never truly been loved. Not the way she needed to be loved.

Perhaps if she'd chosen Tariq four years ago, he might have learned to love her like that. Perhaps. However, back then, she'd been young and needy compared to Tariq's strength and confidence. While he'd cherished her, he'd also been her caretaker. Her love for him had been deep and achingly true, but it had been the love of a girl growing into womanhood. Tender. Easily bruised.

Though her hurt had made her doubt her feelings, since she'd come to Zulheil her love had matured and grown, fed by her awakening emotions for the man Tariq had become. All vestiges of the youth were gone, but in his place was a man of integrity, power and charisma. A man who touched her with tenderness that turned her heart inside out. A man who was, quite simply, magnificent.

She loved this Tariq with an intensity that even his anger couldn't destroy. This love was tougher and gave her the courage to look behind his remarks, to the pain she'd caused. This love gave her the strength to fight for her lover.

From the first day she'd arrived, Tariq had been demanding. Now, she saw that as a gift. He no longer thought of her as a girl to be protected, but as a woman who had to confront her mistakes.

That was the first truth. The second was that she still wasn't loved. And that terrified her. Her naive belief in her ability to reach Tariq with her love had been smashed beyond repair that day before Paris, and she couldn't face that kind of torment again. She'd been rejected so many times in her life that once more might break her. So, while she would continue to fight for her sheik's trust, she wouldn't do it by offering him her heart…or betraying her hunger to be loved in return.

"I think we're getting somewhere," Jasmine said to Mumtaz two weeks later. They were browsing in an art supply store in Zulheina. "He's talking to me."

"Talking about what?"

"Business, mostly." She was drawn to the easel in the corner.

"Hmm, that is good, but what about your relationship?"

Jasmine ran her fingers down the polished wood of the easel. Perfect. Leaning down, she picked up several prepared canvasses and stacked them on the easel. Tariq had always liked to prepare his own, but these would do for a start.

"I don't want to ruin it by pushing." She wandered over to the oil paints and began selecting tubes. Pthalo blue, burnt umber, viridian hue…

"You are waiting for something?" Mumtaz absently added titanium white to Jasmine's collection.

"I want some sign that… I can't explain it." Ever since his return from Paris, Tariq had treated her with kid gloves, keeping an emotional barrier between them. He didn't hurt her with his anger any longer, but conversely, she couldn't breach his shields to teach him to trust in her again.

This lukewarm companionship was simply wrong.

Nothing had ever been lukewarm between them. Their love had been a blaze and their separation pure pain. Even the anger and hurt between them was jagged and sharp enough to draw blood. The sudden change in his behavior mystified her.

"Do not worry about explaining. Simply do what you must." Mumtaz squeezed her hand.

"Good advice, I think." But, Jasmine thought, what *could* she do to breach the wall her enigmatic husband had erected?

"Are you busy?" She peered into Tariq's office. At the sound of her voice, he looked up from his desk.

"You are always welcome, Jasmine."

She ignored the desire to rile him just to get him to respond with more heat. What sane woman would prefer an angry, simmering lover to a friendly, warm one? She had to be insane, because she definitely favored honest fury over a gentle illusion. At least then she knew his emotions ran deep.

Pushing aside those disturbing thoughts for the time being, Jasmine ducked out and picked up the pile of purchases and put them on his desk. The easel she left outside, unwilling to spoil his surprise.

"What is this?" He tugged at the string around the brown paper wrapping.

"A present. Open it!" She moved around to his side and perched on the arm of his chair.

He frowned and immediately curved one arm around her waist. "You will fall in such a position."

"Here." She wiggled and fell into his lap. "Now open it."

He seemed nonplussed by her unexpected cuddling. When she pushed at his hands, he picked up his letter opener and cut the string. His body stilled around hers when he saw the canvasses, paints and brushes.

"I know you're busy," Jasmine began, before he could talk himself out of it. "But surely you can find an hour each day? Think of it as doing something for your sheikdom."

He raised an expressive eyebrow at that.

She smiled. "A workaholic sheik will become stuffy and stressed out, and of no use to his people." She ignored his snort of disbelief. "You used to paint as a way to relieve the stresses of the day. Why not try that again?"

"My responsibilities—"

She stopped him with a hand on his lips. "An hour. That's not too much to ask. And I'll help you."

"How?"

"I'm sure I can do something to lighten the load for you. Filing? Summarizing reports? I'm smart, you know."

He chuckled at her earnest words and his shoulders subtly relaxed. "I know you are smart, Mina. I've always known that. All right. You may assist me and you must also sit for me."

"You're going to paint me?" She sat up on his lap, excited. "Will it be a nude?"

He frowned at her impudence. "Such a painting would never be seen by the world and would be burned upon my death."

Jasmine kissed his cheek, delighted by his acceptance, and scrambled off his lap before he could stop her. "There's an easel, too." She collected the materials. "I'll put this in a corner of my workroom and come back to help you."

She ended up spending the rest of the day with him, reviewing reports. He told her she could leave at any time, but when she saw the amount of work that required his attention, she was more than happy to sit down and dig in.

One of the reports gave her an unwelcome shock. "Tariq?"

He raised his head at her sharp tone.

"It says here that the sheik can have more than one wife." Her brow furrowed.

Tariq's lips twitched a little. "That is an ancient law."

"How ancient?" She didn't intend to share her husband. *Ever.*

"Very. It is a historical oddity. Both my grandfather and my father had only one wife."

"Your great-grandfather?"

"Four." It seemed to her that his eyes were bright with withheld amusement. "Do not worry, I believe I have only enough stamina for one wife."

"I'm going to get this law repealed," she declared.

"The women of Zulheil would salute you. It only applies to the sheik, but the law seems to threaten Zulheil's modern image, some say."

Jasmine nodded, her fears soothed by his practical words. At least another wife was one problem she wouldn't have to contend with. She settled back to work. There was, she discovered, a kind of quiet satisfaction in helping her husband bear some of the burdens he carried on his shoulders.

"Enough, Mina." He stood up and stretched, his powerful body drawing her attention.

She'd been sitting on the sofa in one corner of his study, curled up. Putting aside a report, she stood and stretched as well, loosening tight muscles.

"You may regret your offer." He came to stand by her. "I find your summaries excellent. I will conscript you often."

Pleased by his compliment, she smiled and put her hand in his. "Good. Now let's go before someone else catches you."

Today, for the first time, she'd realized just how many people thought that Tariq was the only one who could possibly provide an answer to their problems. Often they turned up in person. Hiraz and Mumtaz deflected a lot of them, but some were insistent. The relaxed system of government in Zulheil astounded her. However, it appeared to work fantastically well for the small and sparsely populated land.

"Would you protect me, Jasmine?" His smile said he found that a ludicrous idea, given that he was twice her size.

"I think you need someone to run interference. Mumtaz and Hiraz have trouble because they're not seen as royal." She was serious about her observations. "But I am. I could deal with most of what they came to you for, leaving you free to take care of bigger matters."

Tariq was ominously silent. She looked up to find him staring at her, his expression thoughtful.

"I mean, if you want me to." She was suddenly uncertain. A lifetime of never being good enough tended to overcome her efforts at self-confidence. "I know I'm a foreigner…" With a corner of her mind, she shoved aside the secret that threatened to float to the surface. She didn't want to think about that now, not when her husband was looking at her with eyes that held something close to tenderness.

Tariq stopped her with a finger on her lips. "You are my wife. I have told you that my people have accepted you as such. What about your designing?"

"I wanted to speak to you about that," she said. "Would my having business interests damage the royal image?"

He shook his head. "I have many such interests. You wish to develop your designs?"

"I was thinking of a small fashion house. One that markets to the retail sector, but has no shops of its own."

"You will do well." His answer was just a simple statement of confidence in her abilities, yet it filled her with immense joy. No one had ever believed in her.

"But, much as I'll miss not giving the majority of my time to design," she ventured, "I think it'll have to slip into second place."

"Second place?"

"As your wife, my place is here, with you." She didn't

betray the love driving her decision. Until she was sure of
Tariq's feelings for her, she'd keep that beautiful emotion to
herself. Another rebuff, even a gentle one, would tear her to
pieces. "My designing will have to be like your painting.
Something I do for myself, after serving our people." It was
a sacrifice, but one she made willingly. By marrying Tariq,
she'd accepted that the country's needs would sometimes
come before her own. And Tariq needed a partner who could
bear some of the many duties of a leader.

Approval glimmered in his eyes. She was encouraged. It
was time for her to grow up and accept the responsibilities
that came with being the sheik's wife. He hadn't pushed her,
allowing her to do as she wished, but her place was with him.

"If you wish to do this, then I accept."

Jasmine smiled and leaned closer. The slight tensing of his
body was his only response. By the time they got to her workroom, he was relaxed again. She frowned in thought.

"I'll work here," Tariq announced.

She looked up, her introspection momentarily interrupted.
Tariq was gesturing to the semicircle of windows in the southern end of the room. The light was brilliant in that corner. She
nodded and helped him set up.

"Now, you'll recline on this."

Jasmine dutifully stretched out on the plush red chaise
longue that he'd dragged opposite his easel. Before beginning
to paint, he put a cushion under her elbow to prop her up. She
knew that he never bothered with sketches, preferring a light
watercolor outline on the canvas itself.

He was, she thought with pride, very, very talented. She
cherished the tiny painting that he'd given her a month before
they'd separated. It was a Zulheil seascape that he'd painted
from memory to show her his homeland.

"You're frowning."

She smiled. "Better?"

"Hmm."

For some reason, his masculine murmur reminded her of
her earlier thoughts. Tariq appeared to find physical affection

from her somewhat disconcerting. No, perhaps that wasn't the right word, she thought, stopping herself from frowning again. It was more that he seemed to be taken by surprise. He didn't reject her touches, he just didn't seem to expect them. She carefully thought back over the past weeks, and then over the six months they'd spent together four years ago.

Tariq had always loved touching her. Though a highly sensual man, he liked to touch as a gesture of tenderness as well. He'd been autocratic and reserved with everyone else, but with her, he'd been very affectionate. Conversely, she'd been used to the repressive formality of her own home. It had taken him months to make her comfortable enough in his presence to risk even the simple touches that he'd taken for granted.

"Mina." Tariq's disapproving look made her aware of her frown. She shot him another cheerful smile and waited for him to return to his paints. Once he did, she relaxed.

Since she'd come to Zulheil, he'd touched her often. For the first turbulent weeks, it had mostly been sexual and erotic. She'd understood that he wasn't ready to trust her with his affection. But in Zeina, it had been like being in heaven. After spending so much time pressed together on the back of a camel, their casual touching had merged seamlessly into their lives.

However, since his trip to Paris, their tiny instinctive gestures of togetherness had disappeared. Now it seemed that Tariq was controlling the intensity of their lovemaking. Though he made love to her without fail, and took care to make sure that she always reached her peak, something was missing. The heady eroticism of their earlier encounters had been dampened.

Why? Jasmine asked herself. Why would he seek to limit their sensuality, the one place where they'd always been in perfect accord? Surely he wasn't holding against her the fact that she hadn't welcomed him with open arms the minute he'd returned? She almost shook her head to dismiss that idea.

Tariq had apologized to her in his own way, she was sure of
that. They'd made their peace.

Then why? The answer flitted just out of her reach.

"That is enough for now, Jasmine."

Nine

Startled, Jasmine blinked. Only when she attempted to get up did she comprehend how long she'd been in the reclining position. Reaching over her head with her hands, she stretched in a luxurious curve, feeling muscle after muscle relax.

"I'm going to head off to the shower. See you at dinner," she murmured.

Tariq looked up. Desire burst into life in the green fire of his eyes. He stifled it almost as soon as it arose, but answering heat rushed over her in reaction to that single searing glance. So, his passion ran as deep as ever. He'd just decided to hide it from her. Relief that he wasn't truly indifferent to her made her almost dizzy.

"But why would the thought of a shower set it off?" Jasmine muttered to herself. She was in the shower before she figured it out. "Idiot." She laughed at herself. Tariq was the man who'd made love to her in front of a mirror. The sultry possibilities presented by soap and water would be tantalizing to him. They were already affecting her.

It stunned her that she wanted to be in a shower with her husband. She could imagine the darkness of his hand against her sudsy skin, and almost feel his big body pressing her against the wall. As a result of her imaginings, she stepped out of the shower hotter than when she'd entered. Her predinner preparations were undertaken in a state of sexual anticipation.

"I have to entice him into a shower with me," she decided. "Otherwise this fantasy is going to drive me crazy." She would much rather be driven crazy by Tariq himself.

Midway through brushing blush onto her cheekbones, she paused, hit by a thought that she'd earlier rejected as implausible. Her hair was already secured on top of her head in an elegant knot, with a few loose tendrils around her face. Those tendrils now framed her startled eyes.

"What if he thinks our passion doesn't affect me with the same power it does him?" One simple fact that she'd always known was that her husband desired her deeply. His hunger was palpable, or it had been until he'd begun to withdraw. Even at his angriest, Tariq had made love to her until she screamed. She tapped her nails on the wood of her dresser in a staccato beat. "I did manage to resist him after Paris, but that was because I was hurting so much, and even then...he could've seduced me if he'd stayed another minute."

However, Tariq didn't know that. To him, it would appear as if her need was nowhere near the strength of his. To a warrior like him, that would be a blow. It wouldn't just affect his masculine pride, but would be hurtful. He stubbornly refused to believe in her love, but he'd accepted her passion as real and unfeigned. Jasmine wondered what it would be like if someday she began to believe that Tariq didn't want her with the same fervor that she needed him. It would rock the one solid foundation in their relationship.

"Goodness." Her eyes widened in the mirror, bright with realization. "I have to convince him that I want him, or he'll just continue to withdraw and I won't even have our passion to build on." However, the idea of seducing her husband was daunting. He tended to take charge in bed, and his control was amazing. It was annoying, too. If she was going to lose control, then he could damn well do so, too.

"Hmph. Any ideas?" she asked her reflection.

"Do you always talk to yourself?" The amused question had her spinning around in her seat. Tariq lounged in the doorway between their rooms. For a second, she thought he might have heard too much, but his expression was the by-now-familiar warm and extremely irritating one.

"It's good for the soul," she quipped. Out of habit, she went to secure the tie on her robe. Then she noticed the way he was looking at her under his eyelids. If she hadn't been concentrating, she would have missed it. She changed direction, picked up the blush again and turned to the mirror.

When she leaned forward, she was well aware that her robe parted in the middle, offering an enticing view of the rounded curves of her breasts. Or at least she hoped it was enticing. It would kill her if the reason for him keeping his distance was that he no longer found her sexually compelling.

"Ridiculous," she muttered. Tariq's fires were the kind that would burn forever. That was what made him so precious.

"What is?" He moved to stand behind her, hands in the pockets of his slacks. While he normally wore traditional garb, sometimes he preferred Western dress. Today he was wearing a blue silk shirt and black pants, the solid colors setting off his rugged masculine beauty in vivid relief.

Her nape prickled with awareness of his nearness, supremely sensitive to his presence. The urge to lean back and rest her head against his firm stomach was so enticing that she had to issue a firm reprimand to herself to behave. If she gave in now, her beautiful, arrogant, sexy husband would once again have her screaming in ecstasy while he remained in control.

With that thought to spur her along, she leaned forward a bit more. It seemed that a lot of seduction in her life went on in front of mirrors, she thought, in an effort to fight her anxiety over her sudden decision to seduce a man who'd proved so capable of controlling his physical passion. Ignoring the voice of fear, she crossed her legs in a movement that looked unconscious. As she'd expected, the robe parted over her thighs and slid off the leg on top, leaving her practically naked.

"Oh, I was just thinking about some of the recent designs on the catwalks." She waved airily and put down the brush, then picked up the lipstick. Curving her lips into a softer-than-normal pout, she began to smooth on the pale bronze with deliberate slowness. It was more of a gloss, which left her lips looking wet and full, rather than a rich hue. She knew her husband preferred to kiss her lips devoid of lipstick, and tonight was about her husband. By the time they got through dinner, the gloss would be gone, but she hoped that by then she wouldn't need its seductive qualities. Right now, the glistening sheen looked like a brazen invitation.

Tariq coughed and shifted behind her, but didn't move away. Jasmine took that as a good sign, but wondered how far she could go. She didn't want him to guess her plan before she had him safely in bed and at her mercy. She grinned.

"What is so funny?" His voice was rough. She recognized that timbre. Anticipatory heat blossomed in the pit of her stomach. Her heart's beat turned ragged and needy.

"Homosexual male designers and their ideas about the female body," she stated with a decisive nod, proud of herself for being able to keep her head while her hormones were in full riot mode. "I mean, look." She swept her hand over the curves of her breast and hip, lingering just a millisecond too long. "As we discussed before, women are rounded, right?"

"Yes." He sounded as if he was strangling.

"Then why—" she spread her hand on her bared thigh, drawing his attention to the way the fiery curls at the apex of her thighs were barely covered by the blue satin "—are the latest trends going toward boxes and flat, jagged edges?"

When he didn't reply, she looked up into the mirror. Before he met her eyes, she gleefully noted the flush along his cheekbones and the heavy-lidded gaze on her thigh. She thought he'd forgotten what they'd been talking about. Wonderful.

"I am sure you are correct in your view," he said at last.

Nodding in vigorous agreement, she returned to her makeup, aware that he was watching her in the mirror. Keeping a straight face was difficult, but her need to make him feel the same sensual hunger as her gave her the strength. She took her time finishing her makeup and then stood up and crossed to the wardrobe. To her pleased surprise, Tariq lay down on the bed to wait, his arms crossed behind his head. He reminded her of a lazy panther, all liquid muscle and barely contained strength.

Her scowl only surfaced once she was inside the closet. How was she supposed to seduce him with artless ease if he couldn't see her? The bed was placed parallel to the dresser and faced away from the closet behind it. That meant Tariq's eyes were on the bedroom door and she was behind the headboard. Frowning, she pulled an almost-sheer blue skirt off its hanger. The two thin layers of chiffon were just opaque enough for decency, and she'd never before worn the skirt, but today, it was war.

The matching top had tiny cap sleeves trimmed with fine silver braid, and was cut to fit snugly under her breasts, leaving her abdomen bare. She didn't bother to grab a bra because the top was tight enough, and every time she bent forward, the scoop neck would hint at that revealing fact. Walking out of the closet, she put her clothes down on a nearby chair. She almost shimmied into them in haste, before she suddenly understood exactly how sneaky Tariq was.

Far from not being able to see her, her husband had a perfect view of her in the mirror. Her hands went to the knot of her robe. She heard Tariq shift on her bed, and out of nowhere, a belated wave of nervousness hit her. Playing with him was one thing, but could she actually do a striptease?

Before she lost her courage, she undid the robe and shrugged it off. When she leaned forward to throw it across the top of the chair, she thought she heard Tariq's breath hitch. Her own wasn't too steady, but she kept going. She picked up her panties and forced herself to speak.

"Where are we having dinner?" Jasmine slid on the fragile creation of lace and satin, smoothing it over her bottom with fingers that trembled. She snatched them away before he could notice in the mirror, and grabbed the skirt.

Instead of dropping it over her head, she bent over to step into it. She could imagine the picture she presented, and it was making her blush. She hoped the dimness of the light near the closet concealed that betraying fact.

"I had thought the main dining room with Hiraz and Mumtaz, but I've changed my mind. We'll eat in our private dining area." Jasmine didn't miss the possessive edge in his voice. She hadn't heard it for two weeks. At one time, she'd believed it meant he thought of her as an object. She was beginning to understand that Tariq would always be possessive about his woman, even if he loved her. He was simply that kind of man. His possessiveness and protectiveness were traits that she could get used to, she decided. In fact, they made her feel almost cherished.

"Hmm." She buttoned her skirt at the side, picked up the top and turned a little so that her breasts were displayed to him, though her face remained in shadow. She decided that she deserved a medal for bravery. Who would have believed that shy, quiet Jasmine would be trying to entice her virile, sexy husband with such an audacious exhibition? Certainly not her.

The top buttoned down the front, so she slipped it on and then did up the row of five tiny buttons made of white crystal. It was unexpectedly tight across her breasts, which surprised her. However, when she looked down, the line of buttons wasn't distorted, so it appeared that the design required that final snug fit.

Finally, she stepped into a pair of Arabian sandals that she could easily shuck off. Their private dining area was in essence a room full of huge cushions.

"Almost finished." She was thankful that the breathy quality in her voice wasn't too evident.

"There's no hurry." He sounded at ease.

Jasmine wondered if she was mistaken and he hadn't been watching. Walking over to stand beside the bed, she put her hands on her hips and twirled around.

"What do you think?"

He unobtrusively bent his leg at the knee, but wasn't quick enough to hide the arousal straining against the material of his pants. She swallowed a sigh of relief.

"Perfect." His mild tone didn't fool her.

"Hmm, but I think I need some jewelry."

The stroll to her dresser took every ounce of nonchalance she possessed. She didn't even glance in the mirror to check her appearance, not wishing to meet Tariq's eyes and give herself away by accident. From inside the built-in jewelry drawer, she pulled out the fine gold chains that she'd looped over her hips on her wedding day, and put them on. Then she clasped a necklace around her neck. It was pretty but unremarkable, except for the fact that the long spherical Zulheil Rose pendant fell between the globes of her breasts.

"Come on, lazybones, I'm starving." She beckoned to him and pushed through the connecting door to his room. She could have reached the dining room through the corridor, but she couldn't resist the temptation of leading him past the huge double bed. The one in her room had never been used, except for the week that he'd been in Paris.

She heard him mutter, "Me, too," as he rose from the bed. His tone was distinctly bad tempered. She smiled. A starving panther was more to her liking than one attempting to play at being a pussycat.

Her hand was on the knob of the door that led into the dining area when Tariq gripped her waist. Burning heat sizzled through her nerve endings where his hands touched bare skin. His big body pressed her against the door.

"You will wait here while the servants finish."

"It's okay, I don't mind helping them."

His fingers tightened on her skin. "You *will* wait here." Spinning her around, he sealed her next protest with a hard kiss. Giving her a warning glance, he opened the door. It shut with a click behind him.

Jasmine lifted her hands to her tingling lips. He hadn't kissed her like that for weeks. She leaned against the wall because her knees felt as if they'd crumple at any moment. The imprint of his hands on her waist was a living touch that continued to burn her skin.

"I guess I can put up with the arrogance this once," she said out loud, a smile wreathing her face. But she couldn't figure out why he hadn't let her enter the room. Then she happened to glance at the mirror. Her jaw dropped.

She almost ran into the other room to cover herself. The skirt wasn't *almost* sheer. It was absolutely, utterly, scandalously sheer. The outline of her legs was visible with stark clarity, and when she moved, the cloth revealed more than it hid. To make matters worse, the lace front panel of her flimsy panties didn't exactly hide anything, either. The gauzy blue of her skirt granted any watcher blatant hints of the dark red curls at the juncture of her thighs.

The top, which she'd thought sexy but not too revealing, was outrageous in its eroticism. The fabric hugged her breasts with loving care, outlining them with clear precision; her nipples were visible, shameless points of desire against the thin silk. The tightness of the top controlled her breasts, but it also lovingly plumped them up. Soft, white flesh overflowed the neckline.

"Oh my God." She clutched at the wall behind her. No wonder Tariq had forbidden her from entering the other room. She looked like a houri. She felt like a woman dressed to please her master in any way he chose. A wave of apprehension hit her. In desperation, she took a deep breath. In and out. In and out. The added oxygen must have revived her brain cells, because a bright ray of hope stood out from the chaos in her mind.

"He didn't tell me to change," she whispered. "In fact, he said I looked perfect." If Tariq had been put off by her sexy outfit, he wouldn't have been so insistent on leaving her in his bedroom to wait, wouldn't have agreed on her choice, and surely wouldn't have kissed her.

Grinning, she skipped over to the huge bed and perched on the end, away from the mirror. She pasted a bored expression on her face just as Tariq opened the door. He stopped. She saw him swallow, and for once she knew exactly what her husband was thinking. He wanted to throw her on the bed and teach her not to tease him. Except he wasn't sure that she was teasing. And, Jasmine decided, he was too much in control if he could resist that primitive urge.

She jumped off the bed and walked over. "Ready?"

He nodded but didn't seem to remember that he was blocking the door. Successfully fighting the urge to tease him, she pushed at his chest. He obediently moved aside to let her pass, then followed.

Once inside, he didn't take a cushion on the other side of the low table set with food. Instead, he sat down beside her, propping himself up with one hand flat on the cushion behind her. His shoulder and chest pressed against her and when she leaned back a little, his arm provided a hard masculine backrest.

Jasmine tried to steady her breathing, and picked up a plateful of small tarts of some kind. She offered the plate to Tariq. He lifted one dark eyebrow in invitation. With a blush she couldn't control, she picked up a tart and fed it to him. He almost caught her fingers on his second bite. Laughing, she pulled away just in time.

Her husband had a definite glint in his eye, but she was determined that she wouldn't be the only one losing control tonight. He was coming with her. However, attempting to ignore the way the panther by her side was throwing her body into chaos was proving to be difficult.

With a forced smile, she picked up a tart and took a bite. "I've never eaten anything like this." The savory pastry was spicy, with a hint of unfamiliar herbs, but delicious. To her surprise, Tariq reached out and filched the rest of it.

"Hey!" Surprise overcame her inner trembling.

"I told you I was hungry. Feed me quickly."

Jasmine told herself she was imagining the double entendre in his words—surely he hadn't meant that he was *hungry?* She was getting ahead of herself. She mock-scowled at him, but picked up a kebab and fed it to her sheik. He sprawled beside her, seemingly content to eat whatever she chose, as long as she offered it to him. Tariq had never done this before and Jasmine found that she enjoyed cosseting him. Today, for the first time, she'd begun to understand precisely how enormous his duties were. It made her want to fill his life with pleasure, so that those duties wouldn't burn out the bright light inside him, though that same light threatened to make her love for him impossibly stronger.

"I don't think I can eat dessert." Some time later, she put a hand on her stomach. It wasn't terribly full, but she was aware that she might be engaging in some strenuous exercise soon.

Tariq's eyes traveled in a slow journey from her lips to her breasts, to the curve of her stomach. This time she couldn't fight the glow that tinged her skin the color at the heart of Zulheil Rose. The instant he became aware of her response, he ran a finger across the top of her breasts. The fleeting caress made her feel weak and tingly inside.

"We'll leave it here." Tariq rose to his feet and held out a hand to help her up. "In case you get hungry later."

Jasmine almost stumbled when she caught the meaning of his husky words. However, when she looked up, she saw that he continued to exercise rigid control over his expression. If she surrendered now, she wouldn't be any closer to breaking through the sensual barriers between them than she'd been at the start of the evening.

What now? she thought, frantic at the prospect of failure. He wasn't aroused enough if he wasn't ripping off her clothes. She was sick of being gently undressed each night. She wanted her passionate, insatiable and teasing lover back. He led her into their bedroom, stopped by the bed and lifted his fingers to the buttons on her blouse.

Jasmine took a deep breath and pushed Tariq's hands away. They dropped at once, but he'd already half unbuttoned her blouse, leaving her breasts in imminent danger of falling out.

"You do not wish to proceed?" He was painfully correct in his speech.

"Tariq, would you grant me a boon?" The old-fashioned words seemed appropriate. She was dressed like a princess from a fairy tale, or perhaps a sensual goddess from myth, and in front of her stood a dark warrior she had to woo to her side or all would be lost.

"You do not have to ask a boon, Jasmine. I accept your desire not to…" He began to back away. Only the way he clenched his fists at his sides revealed his true feelings.

She gripped his shirt in desperate appeal. "I want you."

His hands went to her buttons again. She shook her head.

"What is it, Mina?" He sounded impatient, more like the lover she'd known before he'd started to withdraw. And he'd called her Mina.

"I just…" She bit her lip. "Would it be okay if I touched you tonight?" This time, she went for *his* buttons.

He groaned. "I've told you, touching me is permitted at any time."

"But I want you not to touch me."

"I do not understand." He was wary again.

"I lose my mind when you touch me, and for once I want to be able to explore you. Please?" She knew asking him to give her control was a risk. But if he said no, she'd just keep trying, she decided. He was already acting with more heat than he'd shown for the past two weeks. She undid the button she'd been toying with and moved on to the next one.

His hand touched her hair in a light caress before he pulled out the pins. The soft curls tumbled to her shoulders in a fiery waterfall. "And what am I to do while you…explore me?" She didn't miss either the slight hesitation or the abrasive roughness of his voice.

Ten

Jasmine undid another button. "Just lie back and enjoy it. I'll do all the work."

Silence filled the room, broken only with the sounds of their breathing. Jasmine bit her lip again and stopped herself from pleading.

"I'll allow you to do this." His hands settled on her exposed hips, his skin warm against hers.

Jasmine smiled and reached up on tiptoe to press a soft kiss to his lips. "Thank you."

He appeared startled by her open enjoyment of the situation, but was willing to do as she wished. She drew back and finished unbuttoning his shirt, then pulled the tails out of his pants to complete the task. His beautiful chest felt as hard as steel under her questing fingers. Delighted by the freedom to explore, she ran her fingernails down the center line of his chest. He sucked in a breath.

"I love your chest." She threw caution to the winds. "Every time I see you come out of the shower, I want to pull you into bed and kiss you everywhere.'' She moved her fingers to his flat male nipples and then ran her nails over both. His groan was music to her ears.

Emboldened by his response, she wrapped her arms around his rigid body and put her hands flat on his back. His skin was so hot it almost burned. Then she flicked her tongue over one of his nipples. His hand moved up her back to clench in her hair. Delighted, she continued to kiss his chest, alternating soft warm kisses with wet openmouthed ones. She kissed her way down to his abdomen until she was kneeling in front of him. When she reached the waistband of his pants, he tugged on her hair with innate gentleness and pulled her back up.

''Mina,'' he whispered, against her mouth. ''Have you had enough exploring?'' His voice was heavy, sensual, encouraging.

She gasped when he sucked her lower lip into his own mouth. He took his time kissing her, bestowing nibbling love bites on her lips before urging her to open. When she did, his tongue swept in and proceeded to taste her with arrogant thoroughness. It was a long, lazy kiss that left her feeling as if she belonged to him. When he released her, she shook her head, breathless and aroused. ''I've just begun.''

She trailed her fingers down the bare part of his arms. His golden skin strained to contain the pure strength of the muscles beneath. Lifting his hand to her mouth, she sucked one finger into the moist recesses. He released his breath in a forceful hiss. One by one, she sucked each of his fingers and then repeated the hot, sweet caress on his other hand, before moving to undo the buttons on the cuffs.

By the time she finished, Tariq's vivid green eyes echoed the perfect clarity of shattered emerald shards. ''Would you like this off?'' He motioned to his shirt.

''Yes.'' Walking behind him, she helped tug it off. The skin of his shoulders was hot and smooth. Jasmine molded her hands over them, captivated by the way they tensed.

The shirt fell to the floor. After pushing it aside with one foot, she shucked her slippers. When he would've turned, she wrapped her arms around his waist and plastered herself against him. "Stay. I want to touch your back." The shudder that went through him vibrated against her sensitive nipples and reached deep within. It was as if a part of Tariq was inside her, touching her in the most intimate way.

Pressing her palms against his chest, she drew back just far enough to appreciate the sculpted planes of his back. Muscles moved like liquid steel under his skin when he raised his hands and put them over her own.

"You're so strong." She blew a warm breath onto his skin, entranced by the way he groaned and leaned backward. His reaction was the strongest of aphrodisiacs. "So beautiful."

His chuckle was hoarse. "It is you who are beautiful. I am a man."

She bit him just under his shoulder blade. "Absolutely, utterly beautiful."

He squeezed her fingers. "I am pleased you find me beautiful, Mina. However, you are not to tell this to anyone."

Jasmine laughed at the mock warning and tugged her fingers from his grasp. Once free, she began to trace the defined muscles of his back with slow deliberation. His breathing hitched, then restarted in a shallower rhythm.

"Would it damage your reputation as a tough, macho sheik?" She began to kiss her way down his spine. Her half-exposed breasts pressed against him, exciting her as much as she hoped the contact was stimulating him.

He took a deep breath. "I do not know this word *macho*."

She started to undo the remaining buttons of her blouse, while continuing to caress his back, pressing urgent kisses against his slightly salty skin. "Macho means you." She grazed his ribs with sharp little teeth. "Strong, manly, very masculine." The blouse came undone. She pulled it off her shoulders and then licked her way back up his spine with her tongue. There was a swish as the blouse fell behind her. Her mind spinning with the extravagant sensuality of the moment, she plastered herself against him once more.

Electricity sizzled between them as skin touched skin.

Tariq's groan was a rumble deep in his throat. Sensing that her panther was reaching the end of his tether, she moved to stand in front of him. Her lover's expression was devoid of disguise, his eyes so dark they were almost black, his desire etched in stark lines.

Aroused beyond bearing, Tariq had to touch Mina. He raised one hand and cupped the warm weight of one breast. She gasped and her fingers pressed into his chest.

"No, please." It was a husky whisper, a sensual plea.

"You will kill me with this exploring, Mina." He picked her up and put her on the bed, aching to claim her. The disappointment that flickered in her eyes at having her exploration cut short fanned the flames of his passion as nothing else could have done. Keeping his eyes on her body, he kicked off his shoes and unzipped his pants.

"Yes?" He paused, waiting for her instruction.

Eyes wide, she nodded.

He peeled off his underwear with his pants. Jasmine stunned him by reaching out and trailing her finger down the length of his erection. His body was racked with tremors. "Move aside, Mina, or I will be on top of you and this will end."

She shifted with an alacrity that made him feel like the most desired of men.

He lay down on the bed on his back, his arms folded under his head. "I think you have about five more minutes," he warned, his gaze skating possessively over her body. He'd thought he could manage the beast inside him, dictate what he felt for this woman, but all he'd done was starve himself. The weeks of enforced calm disintegrated, and the primitive urge to take Mina ate away at his control.

As he watched, Jasmine straddled his thighs. Her gauzy skirts settled around them like curtains of mist.

"In that case, I'll get right to the crux of the matter." Without warning, she wrapped her fingers around his erection.

Swamped with ecstasy, Tariq growled low in his throat and pushed into her hands. Her fingers were delicate and feminine around him, her expression utterly fascinated. Seduced by her delight in his body, he surrendered and let his wife have her way with him.

Encouraged by Tariq's unhidden enjoyment, Jasmine increased the pressure and began to move her hand up and down. Velvet over steel. Burning fire and searing heat. A soft moan escaped her lips. She could feel herself being seduced by his reactions. Tariq's face was a study in raw passion. His cheekbones stood out against his flushed skin and his teeth were gritted against the pleasure. Aching with the need to give him more, to give him everything, she dipped her head and replaced her hands with her mouth.

Tariq's thighs went as hard as rock under her. He jerked up into a sitting position and clenched his hands in her hair. When he shuddered under her inexpert caresses, Jasmine's fear of not pleasing him evaporated. Exhilarated by his hoarse cries, she settled into the task she'd set herself.

Mina's attentive exploration snapped the threads of Tariq's control. "Enough." He pulled her up, his hands rough.

Her heavy-lidded, passion-hot face inflamed him further. With another throaty groan, he hauled her up his body, until she was almost astride him. Then he reached under her skirt and found the lace of her panties. The sound of lace and satin ripping was drowned out by the loud panting of their breaths. Tariq threw aside the torn pieces and touched her with his fingers. Creamy heat welcomed him.

"You're so wet, Mina." His voice shook with the discovery.

Sensitized beyond bearing by their erotic play, Jasmine moved demandingly against his fingers. "Now. Now!"

Tariq didn't argue, sliding her onto his hard length. He was too slow for her. She gripped his sweat-slick shoulders and pushed down, surprising him. He lodged to the hilt inside her and groaned in satisfaction. She saw the look on his face and knew that this time, her lover would be coming with her on the incandescent final ride. He had, after all, ripped off her clothing. With a smile, she gave in and rode him to surrender.

* * *

Tariq drew a line down Jasmine's breastbone with his finger. She squirmed under the light caress. Tariq let her capture his hand in her own and place it over her heart. She was almost asleep, apparently exhausted by their wild mating.

"You were aroused just by touching me," he commented.

"Tariq," she murmured, her cheeks red.

"So shy now?"

Opening her eyes, she made a face at him. "Tease." But she wriggled closer and wrapped her arms around him.

He stroked her back, as if petting a cat. "Always?" Under his hand, she was warm and smooth.

"What?" she asked sleepily, burrowing into his chest.

"Are you always aroused by touching me?" he persisted, even as he cuddled her close to him. The need he'd hidden deep within rebelled against being ignored any longer.

Eyes closed and body relaxed almost totally, Jasmine muttered, "I get aroused just by looking at you. It's because I love you. Now go to sleep."

"Mina, when you touch me like that, I could almost believe you." He knew she didn't hear him, because she'd already fallen asleep. Stroking her hair off her face, he wondered if she would remember her declaration tomorrow. It didn't matter, because he would. The fist that had been clenched around his heart loosened. Maybe being unable to control his feelings wasn't the disaster he'd thought. Not if this was the outcome.

While she slept, Tariq couldn't help but compare the woman he'd seen over the past week to the girl to whom he'd given his heart, only to have it rejected. In his arms, she was fire, unafraid of her sensuality. Yet in the desert, though her persistence had angered him, she hadn't given up probing for the truth of the past. The autocratic part of him that expected instant obedience bristled at her audacity. But there was a bigger part of him that was awed by her feminine strength. This was a woman with whom he could rule.

Since Paris, he'd wanted to take a chance on his wife. Tempted by the promise of the last few days, he found that the urge to let his barriers fall was almost irresistible. He wanted to give her his trust. Except the last time he'd done that, she'd almost destroyed him. Did he dare to try again, even knowing that she still hid something from him?

She had her panther back.

"You will follow my orders. You will not venture into Zulheina today." Tariq slammed the flat of his palm on his desk, the sound as loud as a pistol shot in the quiet study.

Jasmine put her hands on her hips and scowled. "Why not? I've always been able to do so before."

"I have given an order. I expect it to be obeyed."

She blew out a breath through pursed lips. And she'd wanted this fiery, hot-tempered creature to come back? "I'm not a servant to be given a command!" She lost her temper for the first time. After the powerful intimacy of the last few days, he could act with a tad more consideration. "Give me an explanation that makes sense and I'll stay."

Tariq stalked around his desk and put his hands on her waist. Then he picked her up until they were eye to eye. Her feet dangled off the floor. Jasmine placed her hands on his shoulders and refused to be intimidated.

"Has a terrorist organization infiltrated Zulheina?" she guessed wildly. "No, I've got it. Today is the annual Kill-the-redhead Festival. No, no wait, is it Tariq-is-going-to-act-like-a-dictator Day? Am I right? Come on, am I even close?" She pushed at his shoulders, furious at the way he was demonstrating his greater strength.

His shoulders started to shake. She squinted at his face. "Arrgh! Let me go, you... No, I can't call you an animal because that would insult the animal." Tariq laughed harder, his eyes sparkling. "Stop it you...you husband!"

"Mina." His smile was blinding. "Mina, you're magnificent."

That made her pause. It had sounded like a compliment. She looked at him suspiciously. "Are you going to tell me?"

"It seems I have been insulted into submission."

"Hah! Your hide is as thick as a rhinoceros's. Anything I

say just rolls off," she muttered under her breath. "Put me down." He wrapped his arms even tighter around her and walked through the door, into the corridor.

"Tariq, what are you doing?" She glanced around, hoping against hope that no one else was around. His official study was in the main wing of the palace. "My feet are bare. My slippers fell off when you picked me up."

"Then it is just as well I am carrying you." His reply was insufferably male.

She gave up. Wrapping her arms more firmly around his neck, she hung on, realizing that he was taking them back to their rooms. "Are you planning to lock me in our suite?"

He paused and then resumed his ground-eating stride. "I had not thought of that. It is an excellent idea."

Jasmine shook her head and tipped her head back, but she couldn't catch his eye. "Bad idea. Very bad idea." When he didn't reply, she narrowed her eyes and tried to shake his shoulders. "You wouldn't...would you?"

"I must have a way to deal with the bad-tempered hellcat I've married." He pushed through the doorway to their suite and headed for their bedroom.

"Bad tempered!" She scowled. "Me? I think you've got your wires crossed."

"At least it's not my eyes."

"Eyes? What...I can't believe it. You made a joke?" She gave a theatrical gasp that turned into a cry of surprise when he dropped her onto the bed. "Be still my heart."

Tactile pleasure shimmered over her when he lowered his body full-length over hers. He started to stroke her with his talented hands. "Is this supposed to be a distraction?" she demanded.

"Would it be successful as one?"

"Oh, yes," she sighed. "But tell me the truth, please?"

"Persistent little creature," he complained, but his tone was affectionate. His eyes were heavy with sensual promise when he looked at her. "Today is the festival..."

Jasmine's giggles caught her completely by surprise. Tariq

tried to frown her into submission. When that didn't work, he kissed her until she was boneless.

"As I was saying, it is the festival of the virgins." He kissed the side of her neck. "If you'd arrived a few weeks later, you could have joined it. No, that's a lie. You would not have remained a virgin long enough. I almost took you in the car as it was."

"Stop that," she ordered.

"What?"

"Making me crazy."

"I like making you crazy." Satisfaction simmered in those green depths when she shivered under his stroking. His lips curved into a grin.

Jasmine didn't know what to do with him in this mood. In the end, she decided that the safest option was to ignore the gleam in his eye and bask in his attention.

"So tell me." She traced a design over his chest with her fingertip, enjoying touching him through the fine linen. Tariq had never once curtailed her sensual explorations after she'd shown him just how much she adored his body.

"It's a day when female virgins of a certain age make a pilgrimage to a sacred place."

"Where?"

He looked chagrined at her question. "No man knows."

Her interest was piqued. "Really?" At his nod she asked, "How old is this festival?"

"As old as Zulheil."

"And why couldn't I go outside?"

Tariq pressed his forehead to hers and spoke against her mouth. "If you would let me finish, Mina, I will tell you."

Jasmine pursed her lips and slanted him an encouraging look. He continued to speak against her mouth, lips on lips, sorely tempting her to open up.

"I do not know what they do and that is probably just as well. No man is allowed on the streets at the time."

Jasmine frowned, the question stuck at the back of her throat. Tariq read her mind.

"Patience, little hellcat. There is no danger because the married women go with them, including the policewomen."

She couldn't keep her mouth shut. "Policewomen? Zulheil allows its women such occupations?" Once more, the way the people of Zulheil guarded their privacy so zealously left her feeling at a loss. She had so much to learn. And a lifetime in which to learn it, she reminded herself, ignoring the dart of fear that threatened to ruin the moment. Tariq would trust her again and wouldn't denounce her when he discovered her illegitimacy. Maybe, her heart whispered, if she wanted his trust, she should begin by giving him hers?

"I have told you our women are cherished. We protect but do not cage." He ran his tongue over the line of her lips in a teasing stroke. The urge to surrender almost overcame her.

"Why couldn't I go then?"

"Because—" Tariq took advantage of her open mouth to sip from her lips "—aside from the virgins, only married women who have borne children or been married for five years can do so." He spread his fingers over her stomach in an unmistakable message. "When you have borne my child, then you may go."

Jasmine swallowed. The thought of bearing Tariq's child was a dream she hadn't dared consider. And still couldn't, so long as she hid the truth of her own birth. She had to tell him. But not now, not when he sounded as if he cared for her. "How do you stop foreigners from disturbing the pilgrimage?"

"Zulheil annually closes its borders the week prior to this journey. Those already inside have visas that expire that same week. Recalcitrant visitors are escorted out."

"You closed your borders after your parents passed away, didn't you?" She'd spoken without thinking, but as soon as the words were out, she braced herself. Tariq had remained staunch in his refusal to talk about his loss.

He kissed her. It was a gentle kiss full of warmth, but without overt sexual overtones. Jasmine returned the caress, though she didn't understand what was happening.

"Yes," he whispered into her mouth. "For two months, Zulheil was closed to foreigners. Our people needed to come · to terms with the grief and I needed time to heal the fractures."

"Two months? Don't you mean one?" Jasmine stroked his cheek. She wanted to cry with joy. He was trusting her with something important, something that had hurt him to the core. "I came one month afterward, remember?"

Eleven

Tariq's lips curved in a smile. "You were granted a very special visa."

She stopped breathing. "You knew. You knew all along that I was coming."

He shrugged. "I am the Sheik of Zulheil. I knew. Why did you come then?"

It was the one question that he hadn't asked before, and the one that she couldn't answer without giving away almost everything. Jasmine stroked her fingers into his hair and knew she'd tell him the truth. Four years ago she'd been a coward and it had cost her his love. Perhaps she could win it back with bravery. There would be no more hiding the strongest emotion in her heart because she was afraid of being rejected.

"I came because I heard about your loss and I thought that maybe you might need me." Tariq's body tensed against hers. She understood his silent rejection of the thought of needing her. He wasn't ready to make himself that vulnerable. Perhaps he never would be, his pride having been savaged too badly the first time. She swallowed the feelings of hopelessness and continued. "But more than that, I needed *you*. I'd already decided to come long before. I'd laid the groundwork."

"Why, Mina?" His eyes were dark and impenetrable. His fingers dug into the soft skin of her upper arms hard enough to leave bruises, but she was heartened. If he cared enough to lose control over his strength, then she had to have a chance.

She felt tears rise in her eyes. "Because I couldn't live without you anymore. I just couldn't bear it. I woke up each day thinking of you and fell asleep with your name on my lips. I love you so much, Tariq, you can't even imagine."

He didn't answer in words. His kiss was tender and almost forgiving. She didn't force the issue. It would take time to heal the wounds of the past, but she hoped her bravery would buy her that time.

Tariq rolled onto his back and fitted her to his side. "I miss them."

Jasmine took a deep breath and just let him speak.

"I was brought up with knowledge of the responsibilities that awaited me, but my parents made sure I had a childhood and a relatively free young adulthood." He cuddled her closer, as if needing her warmth. "I traveled and I learned. I was given a chance to grow into a man without being shaped by my role. For that, I'll always be in debt to my parents. Any child of ours will have the same chance."

"They sound like they were wonderful people," she dared to murmur, though not wanting to break this fragile rapport.

"They were." He paused, as if debating whether to continue. His next words shocked her to the core. "My mother was dying and she did not tell me."

Jasmine sucked in a breath. "Dying?"

"Cancer." His voice was harsh. "They were on their way back from a treatment when the crash occurred."

Unable to imagine the depth of his suffering, she blinked back tears and asked, "Do you blame her for their deaths?"

He shook his head. "I blame her for not trusting me, for stealing my chance to try to help her. And to say goodbye."

"She was protecting her son." Jasmine understood his mother's actions instinctively, but she could also understand her warrior's pain. His mother's secrecy had rendered him helpless and he would hate that feeling. "It wasn't about trust. It was about a mother's love."

"I have almost come to accept that, but part of me remains angry with her for making the choice for me. Perhaps there was something I could have done. Now I will never know." His voice was haunted. "When they died, I was ready to assume my duties, but not to lose my parents. I felt adrift, lost emotionally. You have to understand, I was an only child, and despite close friendships, no one except my parents understood the demands of our position in this land.

"We are the rulers and guardians of our people. It's an honor and the gravest of responsibilities. For my people I had to be strong, but I felt as if I was enclosed in a cave of ice, unable to feel, until…"

"Until?" She held her breath, waiting for words that she knew might never come, but couldn't help hoping for.

"Nothing." Quick as lightning, he changed their positions, so that she was pressed under him.

She didn't protest. He'd given her far more than she'd expected. His mother's secret explained so much. It hurt Jasmine to think what damage it would have done to the proud and loyal man she'd married, to know that his mother had not trusted him with the truth of her health. Her reasons had been born out of love, but they'd wounded her son. Jasmine bit her lip, unable to escape the inevitable conclusion. What would her cowardice in keeping her secret cost him?

It was her last thought before Tariq pulled her into the heat of his passion.

Tariq held Mina in his arms after their loving, deeply affected by her confession of need. The raw honesty of it was undeniable, but it was hard to trust her completely. While he'd begun to let down his shields, his wife kept secrets that turned her blue eyes dark without warning. Though he'd vowed to have nothing but honesty between them, he wouldn't beg her for this secret. He wouldn't humble his pride for her. Not again. Never again.

He'd thought that she'd fallen asleep, but suddenly, she spoke, "I...have to tell you something."

Keeping his sudden tension from showing in his body was a struggle. He merely moved aside the hair covering her face from him. "Yes?"

She kept her eyes on the bedspread, her fingers playing with the embroidered swirls. "When we first met...I was so frightened of losing you. That's why I never told you."

"What?" He felt a mixture of hope and despair. Was she going to try and give him more excuses? He'd begun to believe that she'd matured, become someone he could trust, but that woman wouldn't try to ease her way with excuses.

"Promise me something first?" she asked.

It was the naked vulnerability of her voice that made his response gentle. "What would you have of me, Mina?"

"Don't hate me for this." Her tone was ragged, as if she no longer had any protective walls, and suddenly, he knew that there were going to be no excuses from this woman.

Hate her? Though he'd walked close to the line, he'd never hated Mina and couldn't imagine doing so. "On my word of honor as your husband." He gathered her closer, tenderness for her overwhelming him. He did not like to see her hurting.

On the sheets, her graceful hand clenched into a fist so tight that cream turned to white and tendons stood out across her wrist. "I'm illegitimate."

She'd given him no warning, no sign of the strength of her secret. "Illegitimate?" In his arms, she shivered. He reached over and covered them with a blanket, tucking her close to him, almost able to see her need to be touched.

"My...parents are really my aunt and uncle. My birth mother, Mary, had me when she was a teenager." Jasmine swallowed. "I found out when I was a child that my parents only adopted me because they received part of Mary's inheritance. They n-never loved me. To them I was...bad blood."

The words came out on top of each other, like a flood bursting its banks. Her fist loosened and then curled again.

Reaching out, he covered her hand and uncurled her fingers, smoothing them out. Her hurt was almost palpable. He'd never liked her parents, but at this instant he could have done physical violence to them. How dare they not treasure his wife, his precious Jasmine? "And you think this matters to me?" He was a little hurt by her distrust.

"You're a sheik. You should've married a princess or at least someone who can claim royal blood. I don't even know the name of the man who fathered me." Her breath was ragged.

That was shameful, he acknowledged, but the shame was not hers, *never* hers. The shame was of the man who'd given his seed to create this lovely woman and then walked away, of the woman who'd borne a child and abandoned her, and of the people who'd asked payment for the priceless gift of this woman.

"Look at me." He turned her in his arms. Jasmine raised her head and met his gaze, vulnerable but willing to face whatever he had to say. Pride in her courage burned in him. "Our people have barbarian roots. Chieftains still occasionally give in to the urge to carry off the women of their choice." He ran his finger over her lips, reminding her of his actions. "A desert male's choice is what is important. And I chose you to be my wife."

"You aren't angry that I didn't tell you?" Her blue eyes shimmered with moisture.

"Of course I'm not angry with you, my wife. I would that you had told me earlier, but I am not such a barbarian that I can't understand your reluctance." He kissed her again, knowing she needed to be physically reassured. Her body felt incredibly fragile under his hands, needing exquisite care.

When she started to relax, he asked, "Why didn't you tell me this when we first met?" Back then, he'd been open in his adoration of his flame-haired girl.

She bit her lip and took a deep breath. "I...just wanted...

I didn't expect Mary to keep me…but I thought after I was older she might want to get in touch. I wrote to her.'' She swallowed. ''She told me never to contact her again. I was…an indiscretion.'' Her breath had become ragged again, her tears barely held in check.

''Then you… I wanted to…to not be an outcast.'' Those eyes of hers brightened with tears, but his brave little Mina didn't let them fall. ''I just wanted to be accepted.''

He heard the important words in that emotional confession. ''Then have no fears. You are accepted. As my *wife*, Jasmine. What you were before only matters if you wish it to.'' Any hurt and anger he might have felt died a quick death under the overwhelming need to shelter her from further pain.

His Mina, his gentle, sensitive wife, had grown up in a place where she had not been nurtured, where her softness had been mocked. It made him furious that this lovely woman in his arms had suffered so much pain and rejection. Knowing what she'd been through, he could forgive her for trying to protect herself. And yet she'd told him her secret. She'd laid her heart at his feet, and then given him the weapons to destroy it. It was an offering of immense trust and courage, and he intended to treat it with the care it deserved.

Slowly, almost shyly, she wrapped her slender arms around his waist. ''Truly?'' At that soft sound, his heart clenched in a wave of tenderness as fierce as the desert sun.

''Are you saying that the Sheik of Zulheil would lie to you?'' He saw a tremulous smile edging her lips and was proud he could make her smile. Mina was his to care for.

''Maybe. If he thought it would get him his own way.'' Her voice was less teary, her smile wider.

He grinned at that. ''I think you are right, but in this thing, never doubt me. You are now equivalent to a queen. No one has the right to make you feel an outcast.'' He would destroy any man or woman who tried to make his Mina feel a lesser being. ''No one. Do you understand, my wife?''

Finally, she nodded, and her smile was glorious. Tariq kissed her, knowing that she'd just shattered the strongest barrier keeping him from loving her, heart and soul. How could he continue to fight his feelings for her, now that he knew what had driven her? How could he hurt his Mina as her family had hurt her, by not loving her as she needed to be loved?

Jasmine closed the door on the last guest of the day and headed to Tariq's study. Since she'd started to spend her days helping her husband, her pride in herself had grown. All her life she'd been told that she didn't measure up, but the people of Zulheil thought she was doing a fine job. And, she thought with a smile, the look in her husband's eyes as he helped her pick up the reins of royalty was magic itself.

"You are looking pleased with yourself."

"Tariq." Jasmine flowed into his arms. Her need to touch him grew daily. "I thought you'd be in your office."

"I have completed my work for today. You make my duties much easier to bear." He cupped her cheek and tipped up her face. His expression was unexpectedly serious. "You are not taking on too much, Jasmine? I would not have you become ill."

She smiled and turned her face into his palm. "Do I look ill or tired?"

He shook his head. "You glow like the crystal of this palace."

"That's because I've found a place where I can belong at last." She was struck by the truth of that statement.

Tariq didn't stop her when she began to walk toward their apartments. He slipped his fingers into hers and shortened his stride to accommodate her steady pace. The ageless beauty of the tapestries and carvings lining the hallway didn't hold her attention while her mind was on things past, but she was constantly aware of Tariq's protective presence. She led them out into the private garden behind their rooms.

"It's like the sun is smiling at the world." When she held out her hands, the thick yellow-orange sunlight shot through her fingers like warm, liquid satin. In the sky, red, orange and yellow vied for prime position in the soft pink glow of sunset, and all seemed at peace.

Tariq tucked a wayward strand of hair behind her ear. "You belong in the sun, Mina."

She turned and smiled at him. "I belong *here.*"

"Yes." He curved his arm around her and cradled her against him. One arm around his back, she rested her head on his muscled chest. They didn't speak until there was more red than yellow in the sky and pink was segueing to violet.

"I know you did not feel you belonged in your parents' home. Was there any reason aside from your birth?"

The question was unexpected, but she welcomed the chance to make Tariq understand the girl she'd been. "I've never talked to you about this. I think I was afraid you'd begin to feel like everyone else."

"No one can control me, my Jasmine. Tell me."

She knew his words were supposed to comfort her, and to a certain extent, they did. However, they also reminded her of the divide that existed between them. Tariq was treating her like a partner as far as running Zulheil went, but in their personal relationship…would he ever trust her again?

"You know my sister Sarah is a stunning beauty." Sarah had the kind of beauty that made people stand in the streets and stare, something Sarah certainly knew. She'd been using her beauty her entire life to bewitch and control those around her. Even her parents could deny her nothing.

"She is cold. She does not have your fire," Tariq stated, as if it were a simple truth.

Jasmine's eyes widened. "Do you really think so?"

"A man would be a fool to be captured by the glitter of false gold, overlooking the quiet, ageless beauty of purity." He wasn't looking at her and Jasmine didn't know if his words were a compliment or merely a statement.

"Sarah never liked me. I don't know why, but it hurt so much when I was younger. She's my big sister and I wanted her to be my friend."

Tariq was compelled to ease the bewildered pain in Jasmine's voice. "She was jealous of you. I could see it when I first met her. As you grew older, you became competition, and Sarah is not one who would countenance such a thing."

Jasmine snorted. "Thanks for the flattery, but I'm nowhere near her in the beauty stakes."

He hugged her tightly. "Your fire burns not only in your hair but in your spirit. Your sister was aware that she would grow colder and colder until she felt nothing. She knew you would burn hotter with each passing year, your beauty growing apace with the unfurling of your wings." He hadn't meant to admit that much, wasn't sure enough of Jasmine to show her that she was gaining a foothold in his heart.

"That's the most wonderful thing anyone's ever said to me." The shimmering joy in her eyes soothed him. If letting Mina see that she mattered to him healed her hurts, then he would risk giving her this insight into his heart.

"Your sister…what is the word?…propositioned me, after I had made my interest in you clear." He frowned at the memory. "She placed her fingers on my chest."

Jasmine's eyes widened. "No."

"I found it distasteful. I simply removed her hand." Implicit was the fact that he'd chosen her over Sarah.

Jasmine remained silent for a moment, mulling over that information. It put a new slant on Sarah's utter viciousness while Tariq had been in New Zealand. She'd known that Sarah wanted Tariq, but not that he'd rejected her advances.

"Tell me the rest, Mina."

Still unsettled, she continued, needing him to know. Needing him to love her despite her flaws. "Because of Sarah and how my parents always took her side, I never felt like I fit there. Then there were Michael and Matthew."

"Your brothers hurt you?" Tariq's dangerously calm voice startled her.

"Oh, no. Michael's a certified genius. He's older than me, and spent most of his life in his lab or with his head in his books. He was kind to me when he remembered my existence. Matthew's just turned twenty-one. We were born…" she paused "…over a year apart. Matthew is the baby of the family. He's also a natural athlete. He's been studying in the United States on a football scholarship for the past three years."

"I don't see what you're trying to say." Tariq turned her around. She saw the frown on his face and knew that he was telling the truth.

"I was so ordinary." Even now, her childish fear that he'd begin to treat her as her family had lay like a malevolent shadow over her heart. "I sort of got lost among those three and their brilliance. I was just…me."

"Even in a crowd of a million people, Mina, you would stand out. I saw you with your family that first time and I saw only you." His voice was quiet but the words roared through her. "Your family did not appreciate your worth. It is good you came to me." With that, he folded her in his arms and dropped a kiss on her hair.

Seduced by his unexpected gentleness, she almost told him again that she loved him, but the part of her that needed so badly to be loved in return stopped her. She couldn't bear it if he ignored her, or worse, looked at her with puzzlement, because that was clearly not the nature of their relationship. As they stood there watching the sun set, a vague sense of impending wrongness worried her. She couldn't shake the feeling that she was going to lose Tariq.

However, as busy days drifted into sultry nights, her fears seemed to grow groundless and without substance, as airy as the desert wind. She convinced herself that she'd been imagining things, and stopped looking over her shoulder.

Days later, dressed in an ankle-length dress of pale green, her arms covered by full sleeves cuffed at the wrist, Jasmine circulated among Zulheil's people in the palace gardens, bathed in the fading evening light.

"Jasmine al eha Sheik." A touch on her elbow halted her.

She turned to smile at the elderly woman who'd stopped her. Absently, she made a note to ask Mumtaz exactly what the address meant. More than one person had greeted her that way this day. "Hello." She attempted Zulheil's native language.

The old woman's wrinkled face lit up. "You speak the language of Zulheil?" she asked in the same tongue.

Haltingly, Jasmine answered. "I try but…I am slow."

The woman patted her on the arm with the warm familiarity that the people of Zulheil seemed to feel toward their rulers. It was as if they were considered part of every single family in the land. She found the easy acceptance wonderful.

"You are of Zulheil. Soon you will speak the language well. My name is Haleah and I come from the farthest corner of Zulheil."

"A long journey."

Haleah nodded and fixed her with a shrewd eye. "I was sent to look at the new sheik's wife by the chieftain of our tribe."

Jasmine knew from her visit to Zeina that Zulheil's system of government was made up of a number of chieftains who exercised local power. In turn, they'd sworn allegiance to their sheik and followed his dictates with unswerving loyalty and even fiercer dedication.

"And what will…you tell…them?" She continued to speak in the beautiful lilting language of her sheik's land, not discomfited by learning the reason for Haleah's presence. For the past month, she'd been on the receiving end of such scrutiny from a number of messengers.

Haleah gave her a slow smile. "I will say that you have hair like fire and eyes like the blue of the sea on our coast. I will say your heart is open and that you will love our people as you love our sheik."

Jasmine's composure fractured. "I…thank you."

Haleah squeezed her arm. "No. I bring you the gratitude of my tribe for making our sheik feel happiness again. The sadness in his heart was felt keenly by all."

Jasmine bent and accepted the kiss on her cheek. Haleah

moved away with a wave, heading for the car that would take her back to her lodgings and then to her home.

A tug on her arm brought Jasmine around to face Mumtaz.

"As your advisor, I have some information." Mumtaz's eyes held an amused look.

"Spit it out," Jasmine said, easy in the presence of this woman who'd become her closest friend.

"Keep your eye on that one." Mumtaz nodded discreetly toward an exotically beautiful woman.

"Why?" Jasmine hadn't talked to the woman, but had admired the way she managed to dress demurely yet still look sexy.

"Hira's family is the most powerful one in Abraz and they wished for her to become Tariq's wife. She was also happy with the idea. Then you came. It does not hurt to know those who might bear you grudges." Mumtaz raised her brows and blended back into the gathering.

Though her confidence had grown since her marriage, Jasmine found it a shock to come face-to-face with her competition.

He'll forget you the minute some glamourpuss princess comes along.

Like a bad dream, her sister's contemptuous laughter whispered out of nowhere, perfectly describing Hira's lush sensuality. That same voice taunted that with women as stunning as Hira around, it was a wonder Tariq had married her at all. Love was a fool's dream. Jasmine gritted her teeth and fought off the ghosts. Tariq had married *her* and he wasn't a man who felt lightly.

Tariq watched Jasmine move about the garden. Her smile was bright and her grace unique. She was at home among his people, a confident woman, sure of herself. No hint remained of the needy child-woman who'd hurt him so badly that he'd had to return to his homeland to heal.

After her emotional confession, he'd made sure that she understood that she was accepted without question or hesitation. It had taken time, but his reward for patience had been seeing her faltering smile grow in brilliance. He was fascinated by her gentle blooming. Four years ago, she'd been a barely open bud who'd been badly mishandled, even by him. It was a hard thing to acknowledge, but he did it with the same ruthless honesty that made him a good leader.

He'd been older and emotionally far stronger. His wife's family had not nurtured the fragile confidence of his Jasmine, and as a result, she'd been easily bruised. He'd put pressure on a vulnerable eighteen-year-old to choose him against her family—an unfair choice. He could understand that childwoman's fears when faced with his arrogant demands, and even forgive her for the choice she'd made. And yet he couldn't deny that he still needed her to choose to fight for him, needed her to love him so much that fighting for him was the only choice she'd ever make.

The last time the choice had had to be made, her family had used her powerful need for acceptance to emotionally beat her into submission. Seeing this new Mina, he couldn't help but wonder whether, if the choice had to be made again, she'd stand firm and refuse to give him up.

Could it be so simple? The difference between the weakness of a child and the gentle strength of a woman? Perhaps he could chance trusting this lovely woman. This woman who quite simply took his breath away.

He planned to go to Sydney in a week, and this time, he decided, he wouldn't leave Mina behind. The woman his Jasmine had grown into deserved to be free. And she deserved his trust.

Seeing that she was having a quiet moment by the small reflection pool in the corner, he strode toward her.

"Why so quiet, my Jasmine?" Tariq's question was whispered against her ear.

"I'm amazed each time I realize that your people have accepted me." It was neither a lie nor the whole truth. Haleah's words had made her wonder just how obvious her love for

Tariq was. If his people could see it, why couldn't her husband?

The pensive look in his green eyes gentled. "You are my wife. There was never any question." He touched her lower back. "Now, tell me what is truly on your mind."

His perception startled her. "Hira."

His brows rose. "One of my advisors needs to learn discretion."

"She's my advisor now, thank you very much," Jasmine retorted. "I appreciate being in the know."

Tariq's eyes glinted with male amusement. "Gossip, you mean."

"Essential information." She smiled in return. "So?"

"How can women say so much in one word?" He squeezed her when she opened her mouth. "Hira's family wished a political match. I didn't."

The practicality of his words calmed Jasmine. "She's very beautiful."

"Beautiful women cause men only trouble." His eyes lingered on her, but it was the tenderness of his tone that made her heart stop beating.

Touched by the subtle compliment, she did something she rarely indulged in, unsure how Tariq would react. Reaching up on tiptoe, she dropped a quick kiss on the corner of his lips. "Ditto for outrageously handsome men."

His surprised laugh drew all eyes their way, bringing smiles to the faces of their audience. However, the royal couple weren't disturbed.

"What does Jasmine al eha Sheik mean?" she asked, since she had him to herself for a few minutes, and the hand curved over her hip told her he was quite happy to be there.

Tariq's smile held an unusual hint of mischief. "You will not like it, my independent little wife."

She tilted her head to the side, struck by his tone. Unless she prompted him, her husband was rarely so playful. "What?"

"The literal translation is 'Jasmine who belongs to the sheik.' The sheik's Jasmine. They know you're mine."

She smiled and shook her head. "They are as bad as you."

He shrugged, unrepentant. "It is an address of honor. If they had not liked you, they would have called you this." He rattled off an unfamiliar phrase.

"What does that mean?"

"It means, 'One who is married to the sheik.'"

She frowned. "What's wrong with that?"

"Strictly speaking, it is respectful, but if a sheik's wife is addressed as such, the people do not believe that she is the one who should stand by their ruler's side."

"How strange. Does that mean you're Sheik al eha Jasmine?"

Tariq grinned but didn't get a chance to answer, because at that moment, a couple interrupted them to say their farewells. Kanayal and Mezhael were ambassadors from another corner of Zulheil.

"I wish you good journey." Tariq's demeanor underwent a subtle change. He remained warm and approachable, but the mantle of authority settled around him like an invisible cloak. It made Jasmine aware of just how different he was with her when they were alone.

Kanayal bowed at the waist, approval on his face. Mezhael clasped her hands together and bent her head in respect.

"We will go back to Razarah with joyful news for our tribe." Kanayal's eyes rested briefly on Jasmine. "I will tell them of sunsets and blue skies."

"All is well in Razarah?"

Jasmine knew that Tariq's question was more an issue of protocol than real inquiry. This afternoon, when the ambassadors had arrived, they'd both been invited to a private meal with Tariq. Her husband had insisted that Jasmine attend, telling her that he valued her intuitive insights.

Kanayal's hazel eyes were warm. "All is well in Razarah."

"As always, you will be in our prayers." Mezhael's eyes met hers. "Jasmine al eha Sheik, I will sing for you."

Not understanding the undercurrent in Mezhael's statement, Jasmine nevertheless knew that it was offered as a compliment. She inclined her head, imitating Tariq's regal action without conscious thought. "Thank you. I wish you good journey."

When they left, Jasmine saw that they'd been the last guests. The others had drifted out, happy to communicate their goodbyes through Hiraz, Mumtaz or the other advisors scattered around.

"Come, I will answer your question in our suite."

"How did you know I was going to ask you a question?" She let Tariq lead her inside the palace.

"You always get a certain determined look in your eye. It is most disfiguring. You should stop asking questions."

"You're a horrible tease, you know that, don't you?" She was laughing, safe in the knowledge that he liked her curiosity and her desire to learn.

"I have you to tell me." Tariq tugged her inside their bedroom and closed the door. He pressed her against the door before running his hands over the smooth material of her dress. "Where are the buttons?"

Tariq's passion was so hot, Jasmine felt scorched. As a result of the inferno, they didn't get around to dinner until very late. Jasmine only remembered to ask her question when they were in bed. She turned in Tariq's embrace and propped herself up on his chest.

"Why would Mezhael sing for me?"

Tariq's eyes were hooded, his expression that of a sated panther. He ran his finger across the fullness of her lower lip. "The Song of Gifting is unique to Zulheil." His tone was indulgent as he explained. "As you know, our country follows the old ways. It is what sets us apart from our neighbors."

"The Song of Gifting." She mulled that information over, enjoying Tariq's lazy but affectionate exploration of her face. "So she's singing it as a gift?"

"No. She will sing it to ask for a gift for you."

Jasmine kissed his fingers when he stopped at her lips again. He smiled and carried on, trailing his fingertips across her cheek to trace the rim of one ear.

"What gift?"

The glint in his eye was the only warning she had. "A child. There will be many such songs sung across Zulheil in the coming weeks." Tariq chuckled at her gasp. "My people have decided that you are the woman to bear the next sheik."

"They don't waste time, do they?" She wriggled up his body until her lips were over his.

"You are young, Jasmine, and not yet with child. If you wish, we will wait."

They'd already lost so much time, Jasmine thought with a pang of old pain. "I may be young but I've always known that I would bear your child."

His expression was suddenly bleak. "Come, Mina. Love me and convince me of that truth."

She gave him everything she had, but somehow knew that it wasn't enough. Tariq needed something else from her, something that he'd never ask for and that she couldn't divine. She fell asleep with a lump in her heart. The fear that had been eating away at her returned in full force, haunting her dreams with premonitions of loss and suffering.

Twelve

"**Y**ou are not excited about this journey, my Jasmine?"

Jasmine turned her face from the airplane window. "Of course I am. Attending Australian Fashion Week will be a wonderful learning experience for me."

Tariq frowned. "Yet you seem preoccupied."

She bit her lip, thrown by his perceptiveness. "I guess I am a little. It's the first time you've let me leave Zulheil."

The hand he'd placed on her own tightened a fraction. "And you will return to Zulheil." His voice was hard, eliminating her misty dreams of trust.

"Yes." She would go wherever Tariq resided. "Will you be very busy with the energy conference?"

His face underwent a subtle change at her calm acceptance of his decree. However, the fact that he'd entertained even for a second the belief that she might defect, told her that deeper issues of trust and forgiveness lay buried within his heart. Even her agreeing to have his child had not rebuilt their broken bond.

"I'm sorry you cannot participate." His mouth twisted in a wry smile. "Zulheil may allow its women full participation, but most of the Arab states at this conference hold different views. Those who agree with Zulheil's approach are helping me to try and change the others' thinking, but progress is slow."

"And to challenge them openly with my presence at this juncture could well destroy everything that you've achieved?"

He threw her a quick grin. "Correct. Even though this conference involves the leaders of the Western world as well, including their women, our neighbors are the ones we must be careful of. I cannot afford to take a too-radical stance and alienate the massive powers that surround our borders."

She nodded, understanding the delicate balance he sought to maintain. "One step at a time. Perhaps by the time I'm fifty, I'll be able to chair such a conference," she joked.

Tariq didn't answer. When she turned her head, she found him staring at her. "What?"

"We will have been married for twenty-eight years by then."

"Goodness. I didn't even think of that."

"Then perhaps you should."

His enigmatic statement kept her company throughout the journey. They landed at Sydney Airport around 2:00 a.m. Going through customs, Jasmine confused her two passports.

"Sorry. This is the one you need." She handed over her newly issued Zulheil passport and put the other one away.

Tariq didn't say anything until they were in the limo on the way to the hotel. "Why did you bring both passports?"

Looking out at Sydney's lights, Jasmine replied absentmindedly, "The New Zealand one was in the pocket of my carry-on bag from when I entered Zulheil. I forgot all about it."

He didn't say anything further on the topic and came to sit beside her, teasing her for her open delight in the night scenery. She teased right back, but once in their hotel room, exhausted by the long flight, she fell into immediate slumber.

* * *

Tariq woke just before dawn. Mina was asleep, her head resting on his chest. He tangled his fingers in her glorious hair, feeling an urgent need to touch her, to appease the slowly healing creature inside him. He'd made the decision to trust Jasmine's loyalty on this trip, aware that she was no longer a teenage girl. What he hadn't counted on was his possessiveness and the frailty of this new accord between them. He'd needed his Mina to himself for a while longer.

He hadn't meant to snap at her on the plane, and had been immediately sorry that he had done it, seeing the hurt in her expressive eyes. But his generous wife had forgiven him. He would, he vowed, try to control his edgy possessiveness. It was not her fault that they were in this country, which had to remind her of her homeland. And it was not her fault that he was…afraid. Afraid that once again she'd make a choice that would shatter his soul. He hated that feeling.

Yet he couldn't have left her in Zulheil. It would have broken her tender heart if he'd forced her to remain behind—one more rejection on top of so many others. He touched her cheek and felt something deep inside him sigh in defeat.

Unbeknownst to her, his wife once more held his heart in her hands.

"I have tickets to most of the shows." Jasmine waved the pieces of paper in Tariq's direction. He stopped in the process of buttoning up his white shirt and stalked over.

"You will be accompanied by Jamar."

She stood up to finish buttoning his shirt. "He'll be bored stiff."

Tariq gripped her wrists, forcing her to meet his vivid green eyes. "I do not do this to clip your wings, Mina. You are the wife of the Sheik of Zulheil. There are those who would hurt you to reach me." His words were gentle.

She gasped in surprise. "I hadn't considered that. I guess I'm still not used to being your wife." She knew she'd said the wrong words the moment they left her mouth.

Tariq's jaw firmed into a determined line that she knew well, and his grip on her wrists suddenly felt like steel handcuffs. "That will never change, so get used to it." He dipped his head and took her lips in a profoundly possessive kiss, his body rigid against hers. "You belong to me."

She thought he was going to leave her with that image of distrust, wounding her. Instead, he turned at the door and walked back to her, his shoulders taut. "Mina." His eyes were dark and turbulent. The gentle touch of his finger on her cheek was an apology.

Carefully, she reached up and kissed him softly on the lips. "I know I am your wife, Tariq. I *know*."

He nodded, an expression in his eyes that she couldn't read. "Take care, wife. I would not lose you." Then he was gone, leaving her shaken by the power of that statement.

Whether it took place in Sydney or Melbourne, Australian Fashion Week was one of the biggest shows on the planet, full of every type of style, color and decadence. Jasmine was entranced, though she never forgot Tariq's words. Did love drive her husband's possessiveness, or something less beautiful? Her mind continuously went over the words.

However, she didn't have to worry about Jamar. Her muscled bodyguard enjoyed watching the women on the catwalks, if not the fashions. He was commenting on a curvy brunette when a hand on her shoulder made Jasmine cry out in surprise. Jamar moved so fast she didn't see him shift. Suddenly, his big bulk blocked her field of vision.

A throaty feminine laugh breached the barrier.

"Jamar, it's okay." Shocked, Jasmine pushed around his side when he refused to budge from his protective stance. "She's my sister."

"Hello, Jasmine," Sarah drawled.

"Sarah." Her sister's beauty seemed even brighter.

Sarah's mouth curved into a smile that was without warmth. "So, what's it like being part of a harem?"

After all these years, Tariq's revelation had given Jasmine an insight into her sister's cruelty. "I'm Tariq's wife."

Sarah didn't hide her surprise fast enough. A bitter look tinted her beautiful eyes for a second. "Well, well. Caught the big fish, after all." She looked over her shoulder. "It's been lovely but I must rush. Harry's probably looking for me."

Sarah turned and disappeared into the dimness beyond the lights of the catwalk before Jasmine could reply. The minute-long meeting left her feeling a confusing mix of emotions.

"She is not like you." Jamar moved to her side once more, his blunt features set in disapproving lines.

"No. She's beautiful."

"And icy. That one is cold."

Jamar's words reminded Jasmine of Tariq's statements. Suddenly, her heart felt lighter, more carefree. Her husband had chosen her. He thought she was good enough just as she was, and that was what mattered.

"How did the initial negotiations go?" Jasmine asked Tariq over dinner. She'd decided to eat in their suite, aware that he'd be craving some peace and quiet.

He ran his hand through his damp hair, having just showered. Under the terry-cloth robe that he'd thrown on to placate her sense of modesty, his tanned skin glowed with health. "It is as I expected. Those with oil wish to keep their position of power and are unwilling to look at alternatives."

"Isn't that short-sighted? Oil will eventually run out."

His eyes gleamed with intelligence. "Exactly. And it is not only money but our world that we must consider."

Jasmine reached across the table and touched his hand. "As an ex–New Zealander, I'd have to agree with you. Kiwis are very big on clean and green."

"Are you?" He trapped her hand beneath his.

"Am I what?"

"Are you an ex–New Zealander?"

She paused. "Aren't I? I thought after marrying you, I gained Zulheil citizenship?"

He nodded once. "Zulheil allows dual citizenship."

"I didn't know that." She smiled. "My heart belongs to you and your land, Tariq. It's home."

He began to rub his thumb in tiny circles across her wrist. "You have no wish to return to your family?"

She knew her smile was a little sad. Even though they'd hurt her so much, they were her family. A lifetime couldn't be easily dismissed. "I saw Sarah today."

"Your sister is well?" His question was innocuous, but his eyes were alert.

She shrugged. "You know Sarah."

He didn't say anything, simply watched her face with eyes that seemed to see through to her soul. When he stood and came around the table, she was ready for him. That night, his lovemaking was tender and careful, as if he was trying to soothe her hurt. She forgot Sarah's barbs with his first touch, her heart overflowing with love for her desert warrior.

Her grip on her husband's strong body was fierce, her loving equally tender, his comments at dinner having given her an insight into his mind. Her husband had been afraid that she'd be tempted by the proximity of her country of birth. He didn't know that Zulheil was the only place that she truly thought of as home, and only because it was his land.

Jasmine spent most of the next day shopping for gifts. Jamar tagged along like a good-natured, if extremely large, puppy, even offering suggestions on prospective purchases.

"Your sister is approaching us," he stated suddenly.

Jasmine looked up in surprise. Sure enough, Sarah was making her way through the small boutique in Darling Harbour.

"How about lunch, little sister?" For once, there was no sarcasm or bitterness in her words, and Jasmine couldn't resist the invitation. Old habits were hard to break and this hint of an olive branch from an always-unapproachable sister was too good to pass up.

Before they reached the car, Sarah asked her if they could

stop in at a travel agency. "Have to pick up some tickets."
She smiled and wiggled her fingers at Jamar.

The bodyguard, who'd been hanging back, moved closer.

Jasmine smiled at him. "We're just going to stop by a travel
agent's office. Can you tell the driver?"

Jamar frowned but did as she asked, taking the front passenger seat, while Jasmine sat in the back with Sarah. As the
vehicle was a courtesy provided by the Australian government,
there was no glass partition between the two compartments.
Mindful of that, Jasmine kept her voice down as she chatted
with Sarah, catching up. When she admitted to missing her
family, Sarah said, rather loudly, "So, when do you want to
leave for New Zealand? I'll book your ticket right now."

Jasmine responded in a quieter tone. "I'll see if Tariq has
some free time after the conference." She wondered if she
could convince her husband to return to the place where they'd
hurt each other so much.

To her surprise, lunch was pleasant. Starved for news about
her family, she drank in every one of Sarah's words. "Thank
you," she said, after paying the bill for both their meals. "I
needed to know about everyone."

Sarah smiled slowly. "Perhaps we'll see each other again.
We're both adults now."

Jasmine nodded. She was no longer the naive girl she'd
once been, and it seemed her sister respected that. And maybe
after marrying Boston blue-blood Harrison Bentley, Sarah had
matured and forgotten her spiteful anger toward Tariq.

Jasmine had no premonition of the sheer wrongness of her
belief until late that night.

She was in the shower when Tariq returned sometime after
eight. When she walked out into the bedroom, wrapped in a
towel, she found him waiting for her, eyes glittering with what
she immediately recognized as unadulterated rage.

"Tariq? What is it?" She froze, suddenly afraid.

He remained on the other side of the room, his big body

held tightly in check. "Did you have fun laughing at me, Jasmine?" His quiet voice vibrated with anger.

"W-what are you talking about?"

"Such innocence! And to think I'd believed you'd changed."

He raked her body with eyes that were so angry, she didn't want him anywhere near her. At the same time, it hurt that he stayed as far as physically possible from her.

"Unfortunately, your sister gave away your plans."

Her head jerked up. "What plans?"

"Your sister commiserated with me over your desertion. She said I had to understand that you could not bring yourself to marry a man like me."

Shocked, Jasmine just stared. When he ripped something out of his pocket and threw it against her chest, she didn't move to get it.

"You did not tell her I was your husband! What were you planning to do after you left? File for divorce, or just ignore your Zulheil marriage?" The sharp pain in his voice cut her.

Sarah had done this, Jasmine thought dully. But she wouldn't win. Her lie was too enormous, too unbelievable. Surely Tariq would see the truth. He *knew* Sarah. "I'm not planning on leaving you. She lied."

He looked even more furious. "Do not make this worse with further lies. The plane ticket in your name that Sarah wished me to give you does not lie."

With shaking hands, Jasmine picked up the ticket, barely able to keep the towel around her. The ticket was in her name, and even worse, her passport details were listed. That was odd, but only seemed to damn her further in her husband's eyes.

"No," she cried. "I would never do this. My family had all these details on file."

His mouth twisted in disbelief. "Enough! I was foolish to believe in you despite it all, but Jamar heard you discussing your defection!"

Jamar had obviously not heard her response to Sarah's

words. She reached for Tariq, forgetting the towel. "Listen—"

"The truth is clear. I have always known your choices. Your body is not enough to make me a fool again. Though if you wish, I can avail myself of the invitation." His dismissive glance broke her heart. He was so cold, so uninterested.

Unbearably ashamed of her nakedness, she pulled the towel around her with fingers that trembled, and tried to reason with him. "Please, Tariq, listen to me. I love you…" She gave him her heart in a frantic attempt to make him listen.

He laughed. "You must think me a great fool, Jasmine. Your love is worthless."

Brokenhearted at the bald-faced rejection, and no longer able to figure out a way to make him understand that her love and loyalty belonged to him without reservation, Jasmine threw the balled-up ticket in his face. "Yes, that's the truth!" she lied. "I'm going to New Zealand and I'm going to divorce you!"

Tariq didn't speak. His face resembled a mask carved out of stone. The rage driving him had been tempered to cold fury.

"I'll go back and marry someone more suitable. I don't know what I was thinking of, marrying you!" She wanted to break down and cry, but some final piece of pride held her in check. If she gave in to the urge, she might never stop.

"You will not leave Zulheil."

"I'm already out of Zulheil! I won't go back!"

The anger on his face should have scared her, but she was past fear, mercifully numb. "You will return," he declared.

"No!" Her anger crested. "You have no right to make me!"

"Get dressed. We are leaving today." His voice was without emotion, as if he'd suddenly tripped a switch. "If you try to make it difficult, I will personally make sure that you get to Zulheil."

"You wouldn't make a scene." The room separated them, but it was the distance in his eyes that broke her heart.

His eyes narrowed. "I will do what it takes."

Confronted with the Sheik of Zulheil, she knew that she'd lost this battle. He had the political power to do whatever he wished. "I have nowhere else to go." The wistful words fell from her lips like long-held tears. "I gave up everything for you. Everything. *Everything.*"

Her only response was the slamming of the door behind him as he left the room.

Slumped outside the hotel door, his control shattered, Tariq could barely think. He knew what Sarah was like, and so, when she'd told him, he hadn't believed her. Even with the evidence of the ticket, he hadn't believed her. Making sure that she knew of his disgust with her for her troublemaking, he'd gone to find Jasmine. He'd wanted to protect her from her sister's maliciousness. Then Jamar had seen him heading to their suite, and had asked if Jasmine had talked to him about leaving for New Zealand. His expression had been dark.

"On their way to the travel agent's, her sister asked Jasmine al eha Sheik when she would like her ticket booked." The bodyguard had started to say something else, but was interrupted when the head of security beeped him. He'd excused himself.

Tariq had felt his heart break with Jamar's words. It was fortunate that the guard had left, because otherwise he would have seen his sheik's composure crack, like fine porcelain under a heavy boot.

Jamar was a loyal guard, one with no reason to lie, especially since he clearly adored Jasmine. Tariq called himself a fool for accepting Jasmine's explanation for carrying her New Zealand passport. He'd broken his longest held vow and had trusted her when she'd said it was an oversight. Even after what she'd done to him the first time, he'd *trusted* her. He'd wanted to protect and keep her safe in his arms.

An image thrust into his mind, turning a knife inside him. Of a tiny woman with hair of flame pleading with him to believe her, her shoulders and legs bare. A woman with shame in her eyes when he'd mocked the inherent sensuality that was her nature. Sensuality that he had always treasured, that he'd taken time and care to nurture.

Another knife joined the first.

He forced himself to remember the reason for his anger. There was no reason for him to feel as if he'd broken something beyond value. Except he couldn't think for the anger and pain blinding him. The wounded thing inside him was in agony, but he refused to acknowledge that, refused to examine exactly why this betrayal hurt with the pain of a thousand suns on his naked skin. He'd survived Jasmine once before and he'd do it again.

Even if what he felt for her was a hundred times stronger than before…and the pain threatened to drive him to madness.

Thirteen

They landed in Zulheil midmorning. Jasmine couldn't help but remember her first trip through the gleaming white corridors. Then, she'd believed that if she loved him enough, the man beside her would grow to love her, too.

Now, she knew that if he could convict her on such flimsy evidence, he had to have no trust in her loyalty. And no love in his heart. She'd failed to make him see that she was worth loving, and if Tariq couldn't see that, then the flaws in her had to be fatal. Battered by emotional storms, her defenses crushed, Jasmine couldn't fight those old demons any longer.

Once they reached the palace, she let Tariq haul her through the corridors, humiliating as it was, knowing that if she fought, he was angry enough to do something truly unforgivable. But when, after pulling her into his bedroom, he turned to leave, she stopped him. She wasn't someone he could lock away and forget.

"Where are you going?"

Tariq didn't even look at her. "Abraz."

Speak to me, she wanted to cry. *Give me something to hold on to.* Even after his accusations and distrust, her heart refused to give up. She loved him. Needed him. And this time, she would fight for him until there was no hope. "Why?"

He did look at her then, his eyes dark green with pure fury. "I am going to marry my second wife. You no longer amuse me. Perhaps she will have more loyalty than you have shown."

Jasmine's heart turned to ice. "You're taking another wife?"

"I will marry her in Abraz. You would do well to get used to a submissive role."

"How can you do this to me?" She prayed that he was only striking back at her because he was angry at her supposed betrayal. Then she remembered gorgeous Hira. Hira, who'd wanted to marry Tariq…and who lived in Abraz. Hira, the glamourpuss princess that Sarah had taunted her with so long ago. Jasmine's worst nightmare had just come to life.

Tariq's beautiful face was cruel with distaste as his merciless eyes raked her trembling body. "The same way you plotted to betray me."

"No! I didn't. Why don't you believe me?" She reached out to grab the edge of his jacket, but he shrugged her off.

"I do not wish to be late." Throwing her another dismissive glance over her shoulder, he walked out the door.

Jasmine didn't go out to the balcony this time. At that moment, something priceless deep inside her broke with an almost audible snap. But she couldn't allow herself to feel the pain, because if she did, she'd die from the wound. Instead, as a self-defense mechanism, she started to plan her escape. She'd been prepared to put up with Tariq's anger, his distrust, even his rejection of her, but this…

"I will never share him. Never."

Sarah's derisive voice seemed to haunt her, telling her she hadn't been woman enough to hold her husband.

"No!" Sarah had probably only meant to cause a fight, but Tariq's deep-rooted distrust of his wife had given her the greatest of victories. Jasmine refused to give her vindictive sister any more power.

Spinning on her heel, she walked to her room and locked the door. She needed to think. There was no way she was going to get a flight out of Zulheil. Tariq would have alerted his men to watch for any attempt on her part. He wanted her to suffer. He wanted to punish her. Previously, she'd let him, certain that her love would win through.

"Not anymore." He'd gone too far this time.

She couldn't take to the roads. The border guards were well-trained and scrupulous. Aside from that, her red hair was a beacon of recognition among the desert people.

"Water." She stopped, her heart pounding. Zulheil had a narrow seacoast and a thriving port. It would be relatively easy to slip on board one of the foreign ships when it stopped to refuel. Sailors were an independent lot, and the harbor authorities couldn't monitor each and every individual movement. Aside from that, they were more worried with keeping people out of Zulheil than policing those wanting to depart.

She knew she had to leave everything behind, so that no one would guess her plan. That seemed to sum up her fate. She was leaving everything. Her heart. Her dreams. Her hope.

Taking a calming breath, she went to the small safe in the bedroom. After their marriage, Tariq had shown her the safe and told her that it would always hold cash for her use. At the time, she'd been touched by his thoughtfulness, but today, she just felt humiliated. Though she didn't want to take his money, accessing her New Zealand savings accounts would immediately give away her plans. Shouldering aside her pride, she keyed in the combination. There was enough cash to buy her passage and support her for a few weeks.

As she turned away from the safe, a flash of silver on a corner chair caught her eye. She had finished the beautifully beaded blouse with such hope, just before their departure to Australia. Now she could barely bear the sight of it. She folded it up and left it on the bed, with a note for Mumtaz. Her friend might hate her for fleeing, but she was the one for whom Jasmine had chosen the material.

Once she was ready, she walked to her writing desk and picked up a pen. Her fingers threatened to shake under the force of her emotions, but she disciplined them with strength that came from somewhere so deep inside, she'd never known it existed before that instant.

Tariq,
Ever since I came to Zulheil, you've been waiting for me to betray you and leave. Today, I'll live up to your lack of belief in me, but I won't leave in silence like a thief.

I love you so much that every time I breathe, I think of you. From the moment we reunited, I had no thought of ever leaving you. You were my first love, my only love. I thought I'd do anything for you, even bear your punishment over my choice four years ago, but today I've discovered my limits. You're mine and mine alone. How can you ask me to share you?

Your pride will urge you to search for me, but I beg you, if you ever had any feelings for me, please don't. I could never live with a man who I loved but who hated me. It would kill me. I don't know what I'll do, I only know that my heart is broken and I must leave this place. Even if I never see you again, know that you'll always be my beloved.
Jasmine al eha Sheik

Dry-eyed, her pain too great even for tears, she folded the letter and sealed it in an envelope. When she'd begun, she'd thought to pen something hateful, hurting him as much as he'd hurt her, but she couldn't. Picking up her purse and the letter, she walked out to his study, the one place no one would venture until his return. She placed the letter in the center of his desk, where he would immediately see it. Her hands stroked the smooth mahogany in a final aching goodbye. In this room, they had come to learn about each other and she'd begun to help him shoulder his burdens.

"But it wasn't enough." Teeth gritted, she almost ran from the room, unable to bear the deluge of memories. Outside, she slipped on her sunglasses while the driver brought the car around. Within two minutes, she was on her way.

The beautiful minarets and colorful marketplace outside the windows of the car brought tears to her eyes. Her sense of loss was overwhelming. This place had become home. The exotic scents, the heavy heat, the bright-eyed and laughing people—they were all a part of her and would be forever.

Just like Tariq.

The docks were bustling. The driver parked in front of the popular waterside café she'd indicated. "I'm meeting a friend for lunch, so you can go elsewhere if you wish."

"I will wait here." His dark eyes didn't reflect his automatic smile.

She hadn't expected anything else. Tariq had been in a rage, but he'd given orders designed to keep her prisoner.

The minute she stepped outside, people waved and called out. They had accepted her without question, these generous desert people. Yet not even for them could she bear to share Tariq. After greeting her people with forced smiles, she made her way into the restaurant and sought out the hostess.

"Jasmine al eha Sheik, you will take a table?" The woman was beaming.

"Thank you, but I was wondering if you could help me?" Her voice was soft, but didn't waver as she'd half expected.

"Of course." The hostess's smile became impossibly wider.

"Somehow, a foreign news crew has managed to enter Zulheil and they've been tracking me. If you could show me your back entrance, my driver has instructed another driver to pick me up. It's annoying to be hounded like this."

The hostess's eyes lit up. Jasmine knew she should feel guilty about lying to her, but she was too numb to care. The back door opened onto a narrow alley. Though the lane was clean, there was a deserted, quiet air about it. The hostess looked around, a frown wrinkling her face.

"There is no driver here."

"Oh, he's waiting down there. Thank you." Before the woman could protest, Jasmine stepped out and began to stride confidently down the narrow cobbled path. Once out of sight, she changed direction and headed toward the water.

Lady Luck decided to give her a chance. A cruise ship was tethered at the docks, there only for a three-hour stop to refuel. In the crowd of European tourists allowed out to wander the docks, Jasmine no longer stood out. The authorities were vigilant about anyone attempting to get out, but nobody noticed a small female merging *into* the colorful mass of humanity.

Jasmine found that the cruise liner was happy to pick up an extra paying passenger, having lost some due to illness at the last stop. As an almost instinctive precaution, she used the New Zealand passport that had planted suspicions in Tariq's mind. Globe-trotting Kiwis were more likely to be present on the ships in port than the reclusive people of Zulheil. Or perhaps she used it because she couldn't bear to see her married name written there.

An hour later, she watched Zulheil's sparkling sand retreat to the horizon. She stood on the deck, her cheeks whipped by the wind, unable to look away. A part of her believed that if she didn't lose sight of the land, the final threads tying her to Tariq wouldn't be cut. Then night fell, spelling an end to even that impossible dream.

The moon shimmered over the minarets of Zulheina, but Tariq could find no surcease from the gnawing sense of loss that seemed to reach inside his soul and steadily eat away at any hope of happiness.

He'd been halfway to Abraz by the time his sense of betrayal and anger had dissipated, gentled by his homeland. Pulsing hurt had taken its place. He'd given Mina his heart and she'd cut it to pieces for a second time. He hadn't quite known what he would do to survive. No one but Mina would ever be wife to him, but how could he remain with a woman who could betray him so easily?

His mind had kept replaying the most painful image—the naked agony in Mina's eyes when he'd told her that he was taking another wife. That he was rejecting her, just as her family had. He'd felt as if he'd struck her, as if *he* was the one who needed forgiveness.

Something desperate and primitive in him had kept saying that he'd made a mistake and had to return home. Searching for any hint of hope, he'd finally stopped reacting and had started to listen.

When looked at logically, without the blindness caused by heartbreak, none of it made sense. If Jasmine had wished to leave him, she could have done so without Sarah's help. Dread had crept into Tariq's body when he'd realized that, but it was the memory of Jamar's revelation that had almost stopped his breath. Why would the bodyguard tell him about betrayal in such a casual way—in the hallway of a hotel, where anyone could have overheard?

Unwilling to believe that the mixture of distrust and anguish in him had caused him to make such a terrible mistake, but knowing deep inside that he had, Tariq had ordered the car to return to Zulheina in all haste. The wild part of him that had always belonged to Mina had *known*. He'd picked up the phone in the back of the car for something to do, a shield against his fear that he'd lost his wife for good.

The guard had answered after one ring. "Sir?"

"Jamar, I was thinking of a gift for my wife and recalled what you said in Australia. Was Jasmine enthusiastic when her sister asked about booking tickets to New Zealand?" His hand had been clenched tight around the phone.

"I heard Jasmine al eha Sheik say that she was going to speak to you about whether you might have some free time. I believe she would enjoy the gift of a trip." There had been a smile in his tone at being asked his opinion. "I was called away before I could ask if I could be her guard on any such trip. I know I ask much but…I did not like the feel of her sister.'' The guard's tone had been of someone expecting to be rebuked for the criticism, but he'd put his duty to protect above his own status. His judgment of Sarah also explained his scowling expression that day in Sydney.

"I agree, Jamar. And thank you.'' Tariq had been barely able to speak. His blood cold with the realization of his incalculable error, he'd returned to Zulheina.

Too late.

Far too late.

The crackle of paper made him glance down in surprise. He felt as if he was looking at a stranger's hand. A stranger who'd crushed the fragile material in his palm beyond recovery, with brutal efficiency. Uncurling those fingers that he was forced to acknowledge were his own, he pulled out the page and tried to flatten it against the dark wood of his desk. The whole time, he knew that no matter how hard he tried to smooth the wrinkles, it would never be enough.

As he would never again be able to enjoy the perfect joy of his Jasmine's love. He'd beaten and battered her heart so many times, in so many different ways, and yet she'd continued to love him, her feminine courage quiet and strong. But even her generous nature wouldn't forgive this most recent blow.

Tariq was prepared to accept that. He wasn't prepared to accept that he'd lost her for good. The woman his Mina had grown into had changed him forever. Her strength, her ability to lead beside him, her glorious sensuality…she was irreplaceable. He couldn't bear to live without the other half of his soul, even if she hated him.

"You belong to me, Mina.'' Only the desert heard his voice. Only the desert sent sighs of agreement on the wings of the cool, evening wind. Only the desert understood his desolation…and his determination.

Jasmine spent the entire voyage secluded in her cabin, eschewing attempts by the social activities' staff to draw her out.

She didn't cry. Her tears were frozen in her heart along with
the rest of her emotions. She just wanted to forget.

Except Tariq wouldn't leave her alone. Each night, he came
to her in her dreams, strong, virile, unwilling to accept her
decision. She tossed and turned, her body covered with sweat,
trying to fight him, but in the end he always won.

"You belong to me, Mina." His hands stroked her.

"No."

"Yes!" That male arrogance was apparent even in her
dreams. His shoulders gleamed in the moonlight, as they'd
done those nights they'd spent in the desert. The desert, where
she'd learned that a warrior's pride could be a harder thing to
fight than any physical enemy.

"Tariq," she whispered, reaching out a hand to touch that
warm, tempting skin. Nothing met her searching hands but
cold emptiness. "Tariq, no!" Invariably, she woke up with his
name on her lips, a cry for him to believe her...to love her.

The liner docked at a number of Middle Eastern destina-
tions, but she didn't depart, not wanting to take the chance
that someone might recognize her. Two weeks passed in self-
imposed isolation. Then the ship made an unscheduled stop
on a small Greek island, due to a passenger's need to disem-
bark because of an emergency. Exhausted by her sense of loss
and lack of sleep, Jasmine slipped off the ship and never returned. It was as good a place as any, she thought without
enthusiasm. And because it wasn't a scheduled stop, even if
Tariq searched for her, he'd be unlikely to locate her.

She managed to find a small garret apartment after she left
the ship. On the night she arrived, she curled up on the bed
and couldn't make herself move again. Thoughts of Tariq
haunted her night and day, building shadows under her eyes
and adding to the weight loss she'd suffered on board ship.
Her mind replayed that final terrible fight over and over again,
trying to find another way, another avenue. There were none.

"It's over. Accept it," she told herself each day, and each
day she woke with her heart heavy with need and her body
aching.

A week after her arrival, she dragged herself out the door, fighting the depression. She was strong, she told herself. She'd survive. So what if half her soul was missing? She'd given that away by choice. And she couldn't bring herself to regret it. By chance, she saw a sign in a shop window seeking a seamstress. Taking a deep breath, she pushed open the door and walked inside.

That night, as she picked up a pair of scissors to begin an alteration, her numbness suddenly broke. It was as if her body realized that by doing something beyond bare survival, she'd decided to live again. With the sudden shift came thoughts and memories and heartache.

Her first emotion was fear—fear that she'd never forget Tariq. And then suddenly, she was terrified of forgetting. He lived inside her, part of her. Paradoxically, there was peace in knowing she would never stop loving him. Despite that knowledge, she avoided newspapers and magazines, aware that if she saw Tariq with his new bride, she would surely lose the tentative control she'd regained over her emotions.

Tariq picked up the brush and squeezed out paint the color of rich cream. Add a tinge of palest rose and he would have the living hue of his Jasmine's skin. A single stroke and one graceful arm came to life. She was almost complete, this creation of paint and emotion. Painstakingly, he began to fill in the details that made Mina unique. Pure sky-blue for those big, always innocent eyes. Even after he'd taught her the ways of pleasure, a part of Mina had remained forever the innocent.

A memory of those eyes bruised with hurt when he'd done something she couldn't forgive taunted him as he painted her portrait. It didn't matter if she never forgave him. He couldn't let her go. He needed her more than she would ever need him. She made his life a gift rather than a burden. She was a piece of his soul, and if he had to, he'd search forever for her.

He told himself that she was no weak woman who would suffer in silence when he dragged her back. His Mina had spirit. She would fight him, and as long as there were words, he would fight for her.

There was a movement near the doorway. "Yes?" His concentration was immediately and utterly focused on Hiraz.

"We tracked down some passengers who saw her on board after the ship left the Middle East. They do not recall seeing her after Greece." Hiraz paused and suddenly said, "I cannot believe she has done this to you again. Let her go."

"Hold your words!" Tariq snapped. "Because you are my friend, I will forgive you that indiscretion, but you will never again speak against Mina. I am the one to blame." It would have been easy to blame Sarah, but Tariq knew it was his own fierce protection of his heart against further pain that had caused this. Sarah had merely been the catalyst.

His advisor's skepticism was obvious. "You? You treated her like a princess."

"I told her I was going to take another wife."

Hiraz froze. Sadness settled over his features, so deep it turned his brown eyes black. "I do not think even my Mumtaz would forgive me such a hurt."

"It does not matter. Jasmine is mine and I will never let her go." Tariq touched his hand to the letter that he constantly kept with him. "Prepare the aircraft. We will fly to Greece. You have a list of the stops the cruise ship made?"

Hiraz nodded. "There were only two." A brief flicker of hope glittered in his brown eyes.

Tariq didn't feel hope. He felt certainty.

Jasmine ignored the impatient knocking for as long as she could. When it didn't stop, she put down some mending and made her way across the small garret, prepared to face off with her landlord. She'd paid up. He had no cause to hound her.

"You!" Her knees buckled when she saw the man filling the doorway. His arms reached out to catch her as she fell. Behind him, the door slammed shut. The garret seemed suddenly minuscule, the light slanting in under the eaves not bright enough to soften the intense darkness of emotion. "Let me go."

"You'll fall."

"I'm fine now." She pushed at Tariq's shoulders. To her surprise, he released her without complaint, holding her only long enough to gauge that she could stand on her own.

Stumbling backward, she wrapped her hands around her waist and stared. "You've lost weight." His face was shadowed with the beginnings of a beard, and his eyes looked dark and haunted, but it was the way his clothes hung on him that worried her. "What's happened?"

"You left me."

Jasmine hadn't expected that response. She shook her head and backed up until she hit the wall. "How did you find me?"

He didn't release her from his bleak gaze. "I went to New Zealand first."

Her heart thudded at that.

"You didn't tell me that you'd completely turned your back on your family to come to me."

Jasmine didn't answer, torn up at the thought that he'd cared enough to search for her. Perhaps, a traitorous part of her wondered, half of him was better than nothing? Immediately, she discarded that dangerous idea. No. No. No!

"You chose *me*, Mina." His voice was rough with the understanding of what she'd done. "You chose me above all others, above everyone else in the world. Did you think I would let you walk away once you'd become mine?"

"I won't come back." Seeing him with another woman would rip her to shreds.

"Mina." He reached out his hand.

"No!"

He didn't heed her, moving to trap her against the wall. The white silk of his shirt was soft under her fingertips when she tried to push him away. At the same time, she hunched her body against the exposed beams of the wall, afraid that her craving for his touch would override her vows to resist him.

"I won't share you." It took an effort to sound strong.

"Because you love me and you chose me."

She nodded, and lost the battle to stop the flow of tears. This close, she just wanted to hold him and forget her anguish in his arms. And the force of his words almost made her think that he believed in her love.

"Mina, you must come back with me. I cannot live without you, my Jasmine. I need you like the desert needs rain." Framing her face with his hands, Tariq used his thumbs to gently rub away her tears.

The pain in his green eyes echoed her own. She tried to shake her head but he held her in place. "I chose you, Jasmine. You are my wife. It is not a bond that can be broken." The fervor of his words made her body thrum in recognition. "I love you. I *adore* you."

"But you've taken…" She couldn't complete her sentence.

"I would never do such a thing," he murmured. "I was very angry with you that day, but I was also hurting. I believed that you had trampled on my heart again. It was the only weapon I possessed and I used it. Then, I did not believe that you cared enough to be heartbroken. I am so sorry, Mina."

"You weren't planning to take another wife?" She managed to get the question past the obstruction in her throat.

"Never. You are the only one. *Always* you'll be the only one. In my heart and in my soul, I have known from the moment we met that you would be the only one. That is why I felt so betrayed. I would never marry another."

· "Never?" she whispered, beginning to understand, to believe. Her husband had turned on her like a wounded animal that day, shattered by her apparent betrayal after they'd seemed to be reaching peace. The broken pieces inside her began to heal under the heat of the truth in his eyes. Unconsciously, her hands drifted to rest at his waist.

"I waited four years for you to grow up. I stayed faithful to the love between us. Do you think I could ever take another woman to my bed, much less into my heart?" His eyes glittered with the power of what he was confessing.

Stunned, she didn't know what to say. She hadn't known

of the depths of her panther's devotion. Her heart seemed to be crying and laughing at the same time, but all she could do was drown in the promise she saw in his eyes.

"Forgive your foolish husband, Mina. Around you, he does not always think with calm." His expression was penitent, but the way he had her trapped against the wall told her that he intended to persuade her, no matter how long it took.

Her husband might be apologizing, but he didn't know the meaning of being humble. Jasmine smiled slowly. She wouldn't have him any other way. "Only if he'll forgive me for making the wrong choice four years ago."

"I forgave you the instant you stepped foot on my land, Mina." He smiled his predator's smile. "I just needed time to salvage my pride."

"And is it salvaged? Will you doubt me again?"

"All I needed to know was that you'd choose to fight for me if you ever had to make the decision again."

So simple, and yet she hadn't been able to figure it out. She touched his hair with tentative fingers. "There is no question of choice. You come first."

"I know that now, Mina." He leaned into her gentle caress.

There was something more she had to know. "Do you think…loving me is a weakness?"

There was no pause. "Loving you is my greatest strength. The assassins sought to blind me to that truth. With heart, I can reach those who would otherwise be lost. I have never stopped loving you." His hands moved down her body to clasp her buttocks and press her close. "Will you return with me?"

Jasmine laughed at the way he was trying to act as if he was giving her a choice, when they both knew he wasn't leaving the room unless she was with him. "Do you promise to be a good, amenable husband from now on and follow my every command?"

He scowled. "You're taking advantage of me."

"It's not working, is it?"

"I don't know." He glanced speculatively at the tiny bed

in the corner. "If that cot holds up under our weight, I'll permit you to take advantage of me." The sparkle in his eyes belied his solemn tone, but before Jasmine could accept the offer, she had to know.

"I love you. Do you believe that?"

Tariq's face was fierce with joy. "Mina!" He crushed her to him. "Your love for me is in your eyes, in your touch, in your every word. Even your farewell letter, which you wrote when you were feeling abandoned and so hurt, rings with the richness and truth of your love. I do not feel worthy of it, but I will not give you up. You are mine."

Jasmine swallowed and laid one fear to rest. There was no room for doubt in the passion of her husband's voice. "Do you believe I betrayed you?" She leaned back so she could look into his eyes.

He laid his forehead against hers as his big body curved over hers in a familiar protective stance. Vibrant male heat seeped into her bones, a deep caress that made her want to melt, but there were questions yet to be answered.

"Once I was no longer blinded by pain and anger, I realized the truth. I did not need Jamar's explanation. My heart knew you would never do such a thing to me." Tenderly, he cupped her cheek in one hand. "I am afraid I am possessive beyond reason where you are concerned, and the closeness of your homeland had me on edge. My fear of losing you turned me a little mad. I was returning to beg your forgiveness when I was told that you had disappeared."

"I didn't want to go," she confessed.

"You will promise to never leave me again. Promise," he growled, no longer gentle and compassionate, the panther tying his mate to him. "Fight, get angry, but do not leave!"

"I promise, but you must talk to me. Promise me that."

He smiled. "I promise you, my Jasmine, that I will talk to you. I cannot change who I am. I am possessive and you will have to become adept at dealing with such a husband."

"As long as you let me deal with you. Don't push me away.

Don't go cold and silent on me. When you do that, it's like a part of me is missing.''

He pulled her to him again, the hand on her nape holding her against his chest. "Forgive me, Mina, because I cannot forgive myself for the hurt I have caused you.''

"I think I could forgive you anything." Her vulnerability to him no longer terrified her, not when he loved her with all of the passion in his warrior's heart. "My only regret through everything is that we wasted four years.''

He chuckled. "Not wasted, Mina. I thought I would give you five years to grow up. I was being very patient, was I not?''

She smiled and touched his cheek in a familiar caress. He turned his face into her hand, his stubble rough but enticing against her skin. "You were. And after five years?''

"You would have decided to take a trip to the desert.''

"I would have?''

"Umm." He leaned down and kissed her, as if he couldn't resist. She softened, she melted, she became his. When he drew away, the masculine scent of him swirled around her, enclosing her in an embrace more intimate than the physical one. "And once there, you would have married a man who has always known that you were meant to be his.''

"So I could've waited another year and saved myself the trouble?" she dared to tease.

"Perhaps I would not have lasted five years. My patience was wearing thin." His next words were uncompromising. "You were born to be mine, Mina.''

The strength of his vow made her want to weep. Tariq loved her, flaws and all. The hole inside her heart closed forever. She leaned up and kissed him, a soft, loving kiss that held everything she felt.

"Does this mean I am truly forgiven?" he asked.

"Just give me your promise to talk to me if you ever feel angry or hurt, and we'll wipe the slate clean.''

"I do not intend to let you out of my sight, so that is a

moot point.'' He laughed when she pushed at his chest and raised her scowling face to his.

''You still don't trust me?''

''I trust you with my heart and soul,'' he told her, his green eyes bright. ''I also need you so fiercely that it would please me should you wish to spend your hours by my side.'' He touched his fingers to her throat in a light caress. ''You asked me a question once. The answer is yes, as you are Jasmine al eha Sheik, I am Tariq al eha Jasmine. I belong to you.''

The raw honesty of his words humbled her and yet made her heart burst. Tariq was proud and strong, as enduring in his vows as Zulheil Rose was in its beauty. For him to surrender to her in this way meant more than could ever be put into words. Her panther had placed his happiness into her keeping, and she intended to protect that trust with every breath in her body.

''Do your people hate me?'' She bit her lip.

''*Our* people are used to the tempestuous women of sheiks.'' He grinned. ''In the first years of my parents' marriage, my mother once camped in Paris for two months.''

''Oh.'' Though the news about their people made her happy, Jasmine was even more pleased to hear the affection in Tariq's voice. It appeared that his frustrated anger toward his mother was passing with time.

''It is I who would be considered a poor sheik if I could not persuade you to return.'' He leaned close. ''My honor is in your hands.'' There was a teasing light in his eyes.

''Come, husband who belongs to me.'' She tugged his hand. ''Your wife wishes to take advantage of you.''

''I would never deny my wife, Mina,'' he breathed into her mouth.

The cot did indeed hold their weight.

Epilogue

There was a roar from the crowd below when Jasmine stepped out onto the balcony, her six-month-old baby son cradled in her arms. Behind her, Tariq put a protective arm around her waist and leaned down until his lips touched her temple. "You are loved, my Jasmine." His smile was tender.

Jasmine stretched up and touched her lips to his. "I know," she whispered. The roar of the crowd was drowned out by the passionate thunder racing through her veins. "As are you, Tariq al eha Jasmine. From the heart and soul."

This incredible man was hers, she thought, without limits or restrictions. Or worry. His birthday present to her had been the repeal of the old law that had made her believe his angry threat to take another wife.

"Our son will be a warrior." Tariq touched one waving fist. "He was conceived in passion."

"Tariq, hush." Her cheeks bloomed at the memory of their reunion on that tiny Greek island. Out of their love and hunger, they'd created a tiny, beautiful human being.

"Our people cannot hear us." He smiled.

That smile made her heart beat faster and her mouth go dry. Every day that they spent together, she fell more in love with her husband. In front of her eyes, he was growing into a powerful, compassionate leader, adored by his people and respected by both his allies and his foes. But what turned her heart over was the way he loved her. The way he saw greatness in her, too.

"I could not have chosen a better woman to lead by my side. You are magnificent." His hand stroked the fiery fall of her hair, unconsciously echoing her thoughts.

Jasmine thought back over the past year and a half. "I feel like I've grown more since I married you than I did in all the years before." Tariq's faith in her had made her dig deep to find the skills he needed in a wife. She'd become adept at behind-the-scenes negotiations, and even better at listening to what people didn't say.

He touched her cheek and the caress turned the crowd wild. "You have also taught me much. Your gentle ways are turning foes into allies. That's why I married you, of course."

His teasing of her hadn't changed. "I told you, by the time I'm fifty, women will be at those conferences."

"I have faith that you will accomplish the impossible." Tariq's confidence in his wife ran deep and true. Mina could do whatever she put her mind to. Look how well her designing was going. His lovely little wife was becoming famous, not only for her diplomacy but for her artistry.

"You are not working too much?" He looked down at her luminous beauty and could understand why their people openly thanked the stars for her. Just as her husband did.

"How could I?" She turned an exasperated face up at him. "If it's not you, it's Mumtaz or Hiraz telling me to rest. Honestly, I could shoot that man at times."

"My advisors know how important you are to their sheik's happiness." Tariq's tone was light, but his need for her very real. Without her, he would not be the man he was today. She had taught him about love so strong it humbled him. He could never articulate all that she meant to him, but he could say, "Thank you." It was a rough whisper.

He looked down at that tiny being cradled in his wife's arms and thanked him, too—for teaching him about a parent's love. The minute Jasmine had laid Zaqir in his arms, he'd forgiven his mother for her choice.

"You're welcome." Jasmine's throat closed with withheld tears. She understood what her desert warrior couldn't say. Tariq no longer hid either his very real love or his need for her. He'd filled the emptiness in her with so much love that sometimes she hurt with the beauty of it.

Moving closer to him until he was supporting their son with an arm under hers, she raised her free hand to the gathered masses. These desert people were her family, her home. Zaqir was a beloved son, the embodiment of the love between her and Tariq. Her husband was her hope and joy.

"We are going in. You are cold." After one final wave, Tariq rubbed her arms and nudged her inside.

Once there, she raised her face to his. "I think we should dine alone tonight. In our private dining area."

He raised a brow, his eyes darkening at her husky tone. "Will the little sheik be asleep?"

"Your son is beginning to be very well behaved." She kissed their baby's soft cheek. "Unlike his father."

Tariq laughed. "If I began to behave, Mina, you'd be most disappointed. Bored." He pulled her into the circle of his arms, warm and strong.

She let him cuddle her to him, their baby between them. "I don't think forever with you would bore me."

"Come then, Jasmine al eha Sheik, let us put this one to bed." He nuzzled her and then kissed Zaqir, his love for their child open and unashamed. "I wish to adore my wife, little one. You will have to be good tonight."

Jasmine smiled in sheer joy. Around them, the rare beauty of the Zulheil Rose glowed with an inner warmth, but between her and Tariq, there burned an even more precious incandescence. As she went to lay Zaqir in his crib, Tariq by her side, Jasmine knew that this glory would only grow stronger with time. Like the crystal, it would endure.

*   *   *   *   *

Silhouette Books is proud to bring you
a brand-new family saga from

PEGGY MORELAND

The TANNERS of TEXAS

*Meet the Tanner brothers:
born to a legacy of scandal—
and destined for love
as deep as their Texas roots!*

Five Brothers and a Baby
(Silhouette Desire #1532,
available September 2003)

Baby, You're Mine
(Silhouette Desire #1544,
available November 2003)

Tanner's Millions
(Silhouette Books,
available January 2004)

If you enjoyed what you just read,
then we've got an offer you can't resist!

Take 2 bestselling love stories FREE!

Plus get a FREE surprise gift!

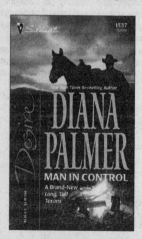

COMING NEXT MONTH

#1531 EXPECTING THE SHEIKH'S BABY—Kristi Gold
Dynasties: The Barones
The attraction between Sheikh Ashraf Ibn-Saalem and Karen Rawlins, the newest Barone, was white-hot. But Karen wanted control over her chaotic life—and a chance at motherhood. Ash offered to father her baby, but only as her husband. Dare Karen relinquish herself to Ash…body and soul?

#1532 FIVE BROTHERS AND A BABY—Peggy Moreland
The Tanners of Texas
Ace Tanner's deceased father had left behind a legacy of secrets—and a baby girl! Not daddy material, confirmed bachelor Ace hired Maggie Dean as a live-in nanny. But his seductive employee tempted him in ways he never expected. Could Ace be a family man after all?

#1533 A LITTLE DARE—Brenda Jackson
Shelly Brockman was the one who got away from Sheriff Dare Westmoreland. He was shocked to find her back in town and at his police station claiming the rebellious kid he had picked up—a kid he soon realized was his own.…

#1534 SLEEPING WITH THE BOSS—Maureen Child
Rick Hawkins had been the bane of Eileen Ryan's existence. But now she was sharing close quarters with the handsome financial advisor as his fill-in secretary. She vowed to stay professional…but the sizzling chemistry between them had her *fantasies* working overtime.

#1535 IN BED WITH BEAUTY—Katherine Garbera
King of Hearts
Sexy restaurateur Sarah Malcolm found herself in a power struggle with Harris Davidson, the wealthy financier who threatened to take her business away. But their heated arguments gave way to heat of another kind…and soon she was sleeping with the enemy.…

#1536 RULING PASSIONS—Laura Wright
Consumed by desire, Crown Prince Alex Thorne made love to the mysterious woman he had just rescued from the ocean. But when Sophia Dunhill ended up pregnant with his child he insisted she become his wife. Could his beautiful bride warm Alex's guarded heart as well as his bed?